T0148544

# THE RETURN
## *of the*
# BAD PENNY

# THE RETURN
### *of the*
# BAD PENNY

## (A Sea Tale of Clichés)

## Les Bryan

# THE RETURN OF THE BAD PENNY
## (A SEA TALE OF CLICHÉS)

Copyright © 2019 Les Bryan.

All rights reserved. No part of this book may be used or reproduced by any means, graphic, electronic, or mechanical, including photocopying, recording, taping or by any information storage retrieval system without the written permission of the author except in the case of brief quotations embodied in critical articles and reviews.

The port of Gaeta and the ship described in this novel are based on my recollections from my time serving aboard the USS Albany (CG 10) from 1977 to 1980.

This is a work of fiction. All of the characters, names, incidents, organizations, and dialogue in this novel are either the products of the author's imagination or are used fictitiously.

iUniverse books may be ordered through booksellers or by contacting:

iUniverse
1663 Liberty Drive
Bloomington, IN 47403
www.iuniverse.com
1-800-Authors (1-800-288-4677)

Because of the dynamic nature of the Internet, any web addresses or links contained in this book may have changed since publication and may no longer be valid. The views expressed in this work are solely those of the author and do not necessarily reflect the views of the publisher, and the publisher hereby disclaims any responsibility for them.

Any people depicted in stock imagery provided by Getty Images are models, and such images are being used for illustrative purposes only. Certain stock imagery © Getty Images.

ISBN: 978-1-5320-7378-6 (sc)
ISBN: 978-1-5320-7379-3 (e)

Print information available on the last page.

iUniverse rev. date: 10/10/2019

# CONTENTS

This book is dedicated to Ehlert, teacher and friend, who continues to teach me to think.

Special thanks to my wife Sue – editor,
muse and queen of the comma.

# GLOSSARY OF NAVAL TERMS, ACRONYMS AND ABBREVIATIONS

**1MC** The general public address system on a Naval vessel.

**Barbette.** Armored cylinder protecting a revolving weapons turret.

**CIC** Combat Information Center; space within the skin of the ship where radar scopes, electronic warfare equipment and fire control are located.

**CDO** Command Duty Officer. The officer in charge of the ship in port when the commanding officer and executive officer are ashore.

**CINCUSNAVEUR** Commander in Chief United States Navy Europe

**CMS** Communications Material Security.

**Conn** Control. The officer with the conn gives orders for the ship's course and speed.

**Crackerjacks** Traditional dress uniform of junior sailors with bell bottoms and a dixie cup hat.

**CS Division** The administrative and operational group of signalmen under the charge of a senior enlisted man and an officer.

**Deck ape** A sailor who works on the deck, often a Boatswain's mate. The term is used as an insult by those who do not work on deck, but can be a term of pride for those who do.

**DK** Disbursing Clerk, an enlisted person responsible for the pay and benefits of the crew.

**Flag spaces** Spaces on a large warship set aside for an embarked detachment for a flag officer (admiral).

**GQ** General Quarters when the ship is prepared for war or other emergencies.

**The Gut** The term used by sailors for that area of a town or city where there are cheap bars, etc.

**HT** Hull Technician.

**Khaki** Working uniform for officers, warrant officers, and chief petty officers at the time of this book. The term 'khaki' refers to all those who are senior enough to wear the khaki uniform.

**LPO** Leading Petty Officer.

**MAA** Master at Arms; basically a shipboard policeman.

**MPA** Main Propulsion Assistant, one of the chief engineer's main officer assistants.

**NTDS** Naval Tactical Data System; a computer system at the time when this novel is set that was an advanced computer system for keeping track of all submarine, ship and aircraft in the area.

**OC** Officer Candidate attending officer training courses before earning a commission. OCs come directly from college or from the enlisted Navy and generally have had no previous Naval Officer training.

**Operations Plan/OPLAN** A document distributed to Naval commands that details actions to be taken during specific events.

**POOW** Petty Officer of the Watch. A watch station in port at the quarterdeck (entrance) to the ship. Serves with the in port officer of the deck or OOD and usually speaks on the 1MC.

**The 'Old Man'** The Captain of the ship. The term is generally affectionate.

**OOD** Officer of the Deck. At sea in charge of the bridge and navigation of the ship. In port in charge of the quarterdeck, announcements and access to the ship.

**Operations Specialist/OS** Sailor who works in the combat information center, responsible for accurate information about the location of navigation hazards, ships, submarines and aircraft.

**Rack** Bunk

**Scuttlebutt** Rumors/gossip. Also a drinking fountain (or bucket for water).

**SM/SM1/SM2/SM3** Signalman. The numerals indicate the seniority of rank; SM1 is a first class petty officer, the rank just below chief, SM2 is a second class just junior to an SM1 and SM3 is the lowest petty officer rank.

**Snipe** Sailor who works in engineering.

**SP** Shore Patrol

**UA** Unauthorized Absence, the same as AWOL for the Army and Air Force

**UCMJ** Uniform Code of Military Justice.

**UNREP** Underway replenishment, when fuel, supplies, mail and occasionally people are transferred from ship to ship.

**Warrants** Warrant Officers who are officers with specific skills who have come up through the ranks.

**XO** Executive Officer, the second in command traditionally charged with administration and discipline.

## CHAPTER 1

# IT WAS A DARK AND STORMY NIGHT

"CLICHÉS ARE PHRASES OR IDEAS or scenes or stereotypes that survive. By their very definition something is not a cliché if it happens or is used just once. Generally in a writing class, certainly one as highfalutin as this Advanced Placement Language class, you will be told to avoid clichés like the plague, that they are overused, to use a finer word 'hackneyed' and, therefore, unoriginal, boring, and even stupid. Perhaps not. Perhaps clichés survive because they express some truth or are warm and comfortable like a pair of old slippers. Certainly many clichés were originally considered clever, even profound. Does a repetition of a telling phrase, of a scene that resonates with most people mean it is bad? Perhaps just the opposite. Perhaps old schoolmarms like me tell you to eschew the use or reliance on clichés, but in fact, the cliché is exactly what is needed. Take the old cliché of a beginning to a novel: 'It was a dark and stormy night.' Maybe it was a dark and stormy night and the use of the cliché drives home a warm, fuzzy feeling that this novel is not going out on a limb, but will be thoroughly enjoyable and fun like your favorite sweater, and the corny first sentence fits the tone of the work like a glove. Other clichés may survive because they're funny or childish or just plain weird. If you want to see a small child laugh tell him or her that it is raining cats and dogs or show a picture of a fat, jolly elf, especially one with a white beard and ridiculous red suit. So I'm going out on a limb here to say that clichés can work, that many survive because they're good, that some continue to be searing or beautiful, and others have become merely fun."

On a dark and stormy day in Boston, February 25, 2002, such was Will Perkins' opening to a lesson in hackneyed and overused language to his Advanced Placement English class. To his students he was a cliché himself: middle-aged, tie-wearing, Ivy League, leather valise-toting washout teaching high school. Some of them groaned whenever he repeated his mantra of "It matters not what you intend to say, but rather what the words actually convey." They were all to bring in a cliché and explain whether it should be used and why; whether it expressed a truth well and clearly, could be used to drive home a point or paint a picture, or ground the reader in the familiar. Or maybe bring back a cliché that has fallen out of use. He was one of those teachers who ostensibly was teaching English but hoped that his 'kids' became more aware and thinking adults. In the case of this lesson, ideally, they would come to see much of their own language, dress and ideas as cliché, but not necessarily bad. He was hoping to see something more than "What goes around comes around," or "Get your retribution in first," or beyond something schmaltzy like "Beauty is only skin deep."

He had not slept well in their apartment in Back Bay, Boston. Most nights he fell asleep with a pile of student papers on the bed and woke early still thinking about the next assignment. This morning, however, he had looked in the mirror while shaving and seen a greying, gaunt man, whose lips were thinner and eyes cloudier than the image that used to stare at him, and he had the uneasy feeling of seeing his father staring back at him. Feeling the coolness of the Italian floor tiles in the kitchen, he was acutely aware of their apartment, a luxurious hideaway afforded because of his wife's partnership in a law firm dealing mostly with labor law and corporate takeovers, and not due to his teacher's salary. He was making a breakfast of poached eggs, toast, and decaf coffee to take to Beth while she read the paper or reviewed her latest brief. He did so before he considered how to drape his thin, five-foot eleven-inch frame or even comb his too thick salt and pepper hair. In spite of spending most of his evening and every Sunday grading papers or preparing for next week's lessons, it was he who found the time to wait on her. He rationalized that he was okay with waiting on Beth since his was a job where he could create his own timelines to some extent and rarely had a boss breathing down his neck.

As he dropped the eggs into the water boiling nicely on their new Aga stove, imported from England, he wondered again whether or not he'd been successful with his near half century. Certainly he'd started out well – good grades in high school in Western PA, where he'd been the backstage guy in school productions, played clarinet in the school band, and even ran a little track. With high SAT scores and glowing recommendations from two proud teachers, he was accepted into Brown, where he'd loved his classes and worked in the library. It was in the library that he first met Beth, one of those small, pretty girls who seem to dress and walk in ways that hide rather than display their beauty and femininity. Never one of the popular girls in school, she saw herself as a skinny, mousy-haired wallflower who was good at school and nothing else. Will still had to construct enough ego in his wife of twenty-one years to cause her to think of herself as attractive. At Brown, she liked to occupy a carrel in the back corner of the stacks, but one day someone else was there and Will watched as she wandered looking for a new home. The next day she arrived to find an official looking reserved sign at the desk. She asked the boy who was always around how anyone could reserve a carrel. "They can't," he had said with a shy smile and glance at her. "You seemed upset yesterday when that guy was there so I reserved it for you." She had turned red, barely able to mutter a thank you, but it was a good start. Although he loved his classes, even then she was far more driven than he and pushing to get into Harvard Law School. He, on the other hand, had no idea what he would do after college. He'd thought about continuing on to get a master's and even a PhD in English literature, but did not feel that he had the insight of some of the better students and certainly did not want to teach. After trying to get a job as a copyeditor, he found himself living with an old high school buddy in Boston, barely surviving on food stamps and a little cash from his parents. One day, he and his buddy walked by the Navy recruiting station and started fantasizing about joining up. Why not? Vietnam was over, but there was still a big drive for people to join the military. This was in the days when the Navy hierarchy still dreamed of a six-hundred-ship fleet. His buddy gave up on the fantasy, but momentum took hold, and in August of 1976, he took the test to see if he could go to Officer Candidate School (OCS) and embark on a new path of "It's not just a job, it's an adventure."

He'd always enjoyed taking tests and this one was especially fun when they gave him pictures of the ground seen from aircraft and he had to choose the attitude of the aircraft. The gum-chewing recruiter said that no one ever finished the English portion of the test, but he should do his best. He finished early with the highest score the recruiter had ever seen. In short, he passed easily but the next question took him off guard: "So, ships or naval flight officer? Can't be a pilot with those eyes, but you can still fly back seat." The romance of the Navy and the tidy uniforms did not include aircraft for him. After all, he was dreaming of some kind of Conradian adventure, or even Nelson, but nothing as modern or prosaic as a jet fighter. "Ships." Two months later, he was in Newport going through the hell of the first week, when the OCs a few months ahead of him tried to make life difficult enough for him to wash out.

Beth, meanwhile, was distraught. She had always dreamed of his becoming a great writer or professor, and this craziness of joining the Navy she saw as a betrayal of his intellect, and more importantly, her. She was on her way to California to Berkeley for law school and saw no reason why he should not tag along. In the optimism of youth, he saw no reason why things still couldn't work out and surely he could get assigned to a ship on the West Coast.

Such were his reflections as he kissed her good morning and placed the tray on the bedside cabinet and went downstairs to fix some oatmeal for himself. Beth was the same age as Will but looked younger, due in part to a good exercise regime, just one aspect of her tightly organized and controlled, almost ascetic lifestyle. Part of her beauty, too, besides a girlish figure on a slight five-foot four-inch frame, was that at moments like first light she still looked like a wide-eyed innocent. That was, of course, before she donned her stylish lawyer suit, discrete make-up, intimidating jewelry, and set her jaw for work.

Beth had not always been as practiced at making her 'advocate's uniform.' When she went to Berkeley, she began to study lawyers and how they conducted themselves as well as the law. Much of this she owed to Will. After weeks of small talk and clumsy flirtation in the library at Brown, he finally asked her to lunch, then to dinner, then to a Strauss concert, and then to overcome her shyness and spend the night with him. They were happy as any young couple in love would be, but they also began to see themselves as people with the ability to make their dreams of passion, marriage, and children come true. Then came law school interviews when Beth, or so she told the tale, failed miserably by reprising her slump-shouldered, monosyllabic persona that came most naturally, if not comfortably, to her. When she came out of the interview, she dream-walked to Harvard Yard where she had arranged to meet Will. She saw immediately in his tight lips and the way he peered at her that he was not going to offer her the solace she wanted. Her eyes watered, and he softened when she put her head on his chest inviting him to hold her. He did not hug her, but led her by her left hand to a bench where he shifted so he could look straight at her. Determined to provide both what she wanted and needed, he began, "Please tell me what went wrong."

"It's me. I went wrong." She had managed to look at him with her head slightly tilted to the left, and her voice was clear, if quiet. "I went into myself and found someone with no confidence, no story to tell, nothing but 'yes sirs.'"

Will knew this 'yes sir' girl well, but he also knew a tough, academic, driven woman who had far more ambition than he. "What did he ask?"

"He asked why I wanted to be a lawyer."

"And you said?"

"Some drivel about it always being my dream and I like finding details and organizing a case."

"Jesus! So why do you want to be a lawyer?" His tone was harsh and he intended to break her out of her sorry state. He did.

"You know why I want to be a lawyer. Can't you just be nice and be there for me?"

"Sure. Why do you want to be a lawyer? You don't act like one and you don't act like you want to be a lawyer." Will had hoped he wasn't skating on too thin ice.

Beth was finally angry and lashed out. "I want to be a lawyer, you prick, because I love the law. I love its detail, and its necessity. There's not a whole lot that really makes sense to me, but one thing is the absolute civilizing effect of laws upon society. And someone with a good eye for detail and an excellent memory for cases and precedents belongs in a law firm."

"No, shit, says the prick," laughing. "Next interview pretend that someone is trying to take something away from you; make them understand that you've got some fire in your belly as you just did with me."

Beth took a long time to forgive Will for being so unsympathetic, but twenty-eight years later, she felt that she still owed him.

It was February and the colors on Boston Common were turning into a beautiful New England late winter's day. From their window, they could see the Embankment, that impressive park that was raised out of the mud like all the buildings there that sat on what was once seabed. Even now they relied on the huge beams that held up the neighborhood to remain wet so they would not rot and pull their load back into the ground. The sky was red. *Ah*, he thought, *red sky at morning, sailors take warning.* The phone rang.

"Hello," he answered with his usual diffidence.

A Midwestern voice, full of an almost contemptuous sneer replied, "Yeah, hello, sounds like I got the right number. How are ya', Lieutenant Perkins?"

Later, Will would wonder how long he stood there with memories flashing like the finale of a Fourth of July fireworks celebration. Although he only put ships on the West Coast on his "dream sheet" for assignments, he'd been ordered to the *USS Utica* (CG 15), the Sixth Fleet flagship, in Gaeta, Italy. After a few days in comm school to learn how to be a CMS custodian (in charge of the security, distribution, and destruction of cryptologic cards), he found himself in a junior officers' stateroom with five other ensigns and assigned as CS division officer, which was the signalmen, and as CMS custodian for the *Utica* and embarked flag (Sixth Fleet Admiral). The signalmen were an unimpressive group of fourteen, six petty officers and eight seamen, most of whom never wanted to be on the signal bridge. He especially enjoyed his CMS job since he could hide away in his walk-in safe and methodically keep all the records of the hundreds of cards and codes he distributed every month. He even enjoyed the monthly burn run of all the old crypto cards dragging the burn bags, which looked like oversized paper grocery sacks, down the ship's ladders to an incinerator and then watching the red hot papers burst into flame and and ashes and fly securely away.

As for the division, he really didn't have to do much but left things to SM1 Mooney. The division had no chief so Mooney was in charge. Will liked his good humor and swaggering sailor persona. He was one of those sailors who had married early and had three lively kids, but who spent his time talking about his exploits in the last port's gut (unsavory sailor ghetto) or tales from guts he had known from Olongapo to Norfolk. He inhabited that sailor world that hardly exists now of loving to be at sea, of feeling more at home on a ship than anywhere, and leaving his home only to see how much he could drink and how many women he could woo or pay for without getting busted again. One of his favorite tales of how unworldly he was, except in the ways of how to survive and excel in gut crawling, was from his days serving on a destroyer out of Piraeus. His grandfather died and he was due to go home on emergency leave, but his division officer would not sign his leave chit unless Mooney could show a ticket for visiting the Parthenon and convince him that he had actually gone to visit the gods. Mooney complied and waxed lyrical about the Greek goddesses, both those revered in the monuments and their descendants manning the ticket booths. Mooney's division officer signed the chit, saying, "Good, now when your grandmother asks you about Athens, you'll have something to tell her other than the unique flexibility of Consuela from Majorca."

The signalmen were on a three section watch bill at sea; the other two sections were headed by second class petty officers, Will's favorite two sailors in the division. Davis was a draft dodger, having joined the Navy to keep from getting drafted into the Army. He was hardly career Navy material, but he was smart and honest and working on a degree. Dragila, on the other hand, did want to be a lifer, but he hardly followed Mooney's example of marriage to the ship. He had courted a local Italian girl, learned to speak reasonable Italian, and now spent every moment he could with his wife and her family. As the others in the division put it, Dragila had gone native. He always took as many watches in other ports as possible in exchange for free time in Gaeta.

Then there were the third classes, but only one of them flashed into full relief before Will. This was SM3 Mote, a boy from a small Missouri town, who nevertheless seemed to be born streetwise. He was cocky, blond, freckled, and vicious. Never overtly insubordinate or disrespectful, he nevertheless caused most officers to feel uneasy around him, as if a hateful chill was giving them goosebumps. Mote loved to bait Will by telling him tales that his division officer could not approve of or desire to hear. Mote's favorite was his tale of screwing the smart boy in his high school class. Mote and his hood friends convinced this poor kid to hold up a liquor store. The scholar did so, as Mote told the tale, because Mote was scarier than all the pigs in his home town. The plan was for the pigeon to get the cash and then hide it in a trash can behind the principal's house on Third Street. All went to plan, but the poor, smart kid did not know until it was too late that Mote's real scheme was to wait for a reward to be offered for information, and then turn in his pigeon as well as the money, minus a few hundred dollars. Mote was written about in the town journal as a hero, while the scholar got a suspended sentence because of his clean record and age of seventeen. Mote would tell that story over and over to Will who felt more and more uncomfortable hearing the same tale, with its underlying threat of intimidation. Will finally asked Mote if he didn't have any other stories.

"Oh, sure, lieutenant. Last time we were in Toulon, I made four hundred bucks."

"Please tell me this was nothing illegal."

"Not sure. See, the thing is my very good friend is a boatswain's mate – fuckin' animal named Jervis."

"I have had the pleasure of having him as my petty officer of the watch."

"Some mean bastard, huh?" Mote had grinned. "So, we're in this bar and Jervis starts telling the Brit sailors in there that their ships look like shit and their uniforms are stupid. This big ass, incomprehensible guy starts shoving Jervis, and next thing you know the big Greek who runs the place has pushed them both into the street. Opportunity, thinks I. 'Wait, wait, wait,' says I, 'I got fifty dollars or whatever the Brit equivalent is that Jervis here puts mush mouth here on the ground in one minute or less.' I get eight bets while the two apes shove at one another, and right when the last bet is coming to me, Jervis suckers this guy with a right uppercut. Lifts the big bastard right off his feet and he lands, thud, in the street, bleeding all over the place. So, then Jervis looks around and says 'All these motherfuckers paid up?' 'Sure,' I says, give him a fifty and we drink ourselves shitless."

"Uh, who is this, please?"

"Ah, come on, lieutenant, who else would drop a call out of nowhere? Who else do you owe big time?"

# CHAPTER 2

# THOSE WHO CAN'T, TEACH

WILL'S CLASSROOM WAS A MONUMENT to tradition. Conscious that of all the senses, it is smell that most triggers memories, he appreciated the odor of chalk lingering in his room. Like most of the comfortable parts of his life, he wanted the familiar and tried. This was not so much because he was averse to change (although he did look askance at what he thought were fads or ephemeral philosophies), but more because he had learned to appreciate tradition and well worn truths; he lived well and wanted to share his good fortune. The wooden desks were in neat rows, the walls sparsely decorated with advertisements for Shakespearean productions, and, of course, his blackboard's surface was rubbed grey. His one dip into a modern classroom was a computer connected to an in-focus machine so he could scan and project student writing. A more personal and unstated reason for the projector was that he found using a keyboard faster and certainly less humiliatingthan scratching out his laughably illegible cursive.

The class had performed well with their assignment. They'd even managed to drag out some delightfully old and strange sayings like "don't put all your eggs in one basket," "the pot calling the kettle black," and "between a rock and a hard place." Naturally, there were clichés to match his class's age like "stupid is as stupid does" and "don't get a tattoo of someone's name if you haven't known them for two years," and some phrases that might one day turn into clichés, but were new to Will like "ugly is as ugly does."

Two of the students offered to read their quick write essays about a cliché. Chris, one of those easily intelligent boys whose usual essays were about football, had chosen "If it ain't broke, don't fix it," and used the phrase as an impetus for a diatribe against all the educational and sport 'innovations' he had suffered during his life. He considered that his education had suffered as result of teachers trying out the latest fads from outcomes-based education to learning math with different base systems.

His coup was his use of yet another cliché: "Counting in base two is a bit like getting to second base – lots of hard work and some promise of good things to come, but finally frustrating and forgettable."

Charlotte, surprisingly, also volunteered. She was one of those demure and diffident girls who have no idea that they will be beautiful in their twenties once they have learned to smile and walk without as much self-consciousness. Tall and thin, she tended to stoop and to wear unflattering, loose clothing that matched her unstyled shoulder length hair. Without doubt, she was the kind of girl whom teachers wonder about later, imagining the first time someone told her she was beautiful. She was certainly one of Will's favorites, and he lied to himself that the physical attraction he felt for her did not color his responses to her work. He was glad that he had reached an age when the girls no longer found him attractive and he could laugh with Beth about his early years of teaching when some girls, especially the wallflowers, sent signals that he lived large in their fantasies. He had been unaware at the time, and only with age and a few sessions of hysterical laughter from Beth, did he finally accept that a teenage girl might find him attractive.

As expected from Charlotte, she had dragged up a phrase that was cliché a full fifty years earlier, but which none of the others had heard. "You're not made of sugar, you won't melt" was a favorite saying of her English grandmother, and Charlotte used it as an example of a metaphor that could cause one to think beyond his or her immediate limitations and self-concept. "While we often think that our tasks and relationships are impossible, we should consider the real consequences, the 'bottom line' to 'coin a phrase.' Survival of troublesome situations is often easier than we anticipate and we find that we are not made of sugar and persevere and survive perfectly well, even in the rain. I think of this phrase especially when given an assignment I don't truly understand and yet must assume understanding. As often as not, the process of working the problem or issue causes a revelation of the nature of my undertaking. Just give it 'the old college try' and often things will 'come up trumps.'" Although Will was the only one laughing at Charlotte's cheeky use of other clichés, the class altogether understood that her essay was about risk taking and some saw Charlotte in a new light, since most of them thought she was afraid of her own shadow.

Will took over where Charlotte stopped. "So, why think about clichés or even know what the word means? For one thing, we are surrounded by clichés and maybe our own ways of dressing in a white shirt and tie or jeans and a t-shirt allow us to hide behind a stereotype and not have to even think about a style or syntax or interest that would cause us to take a risk. Maybe most of us do believe we are made of sugar and the unfamiliar will melt us like the witch in *The Wizard of Oz*. So, today, for a change, I'm going to give you the answers or at least my answers and I am going to tell you about the cliché who is your teacher. Clichés survive because they encapsulate some little truth or perhaps a prejudice, and they are confined to the research books when they no longer strike any chord within us or cause us to nod with humor or recognition. Some of those old sayings are uncomfortable, like "Never marry a girl without knowing her mother for she will turn into her mother." That's a little ditty that's as upsetting for the girl as it is for the boy."

The class twittered a bit at that point, but most of them were watching Mr. Perkins closely. They had never heard the undertone of passion in his voice quite like this and he was speaking louder and with more animation than usual. He wasn't wearing a tie and he always wore ties, and his brown hair, streaked with grey at the temples, was uncombed. With his white shirtsleeves rolled up, he seemed thinner than usual. That intense stare was lacking any hint of humor. Something was up and the more cynical among them feared an impossible assignment coming their way.

"As for me, like most teachers, I have had to stare at the possible truth of 'those who can do; those who can't, teach.' My mother had great dreams for me of becoming a lawyer. My wife thinks I should be a writer. My brother thinks I should never have left the Navy, but here I am wondering if my life is just a poor attempt to make up for ambitions gone sour, that I do nothing but 'cast pearls before swine,' but do nothing good for the swine – that's all of you in this cliché, by the way – but only try to find a little respect for myself.

"So, clichés can come to haunt you. They are a kind of poor man's poetry, a boiled down truth or observation that rests on bones and souls far beyond their simple wit. Take 'you can't put in what God left out.' That's often said of athletes whose skills cannot exceed their capacity, but what about the rest of us? What did God leave out? Did he leave out some basic goodness that will condemn us to continually try to break the rules that bind us together in society? Did he leave out the emotional intelligence to let us know when we are hurting someone? Or is it only males who are lacking? (*A twitter from the girls.*) Has this old dog lost the capacity to learn any new tricks? Am I caught on a merry-go-round, doomed to repeat the same clichés forever? Do we all just put on brave faces because we are afraid of our own shadows or perhaps of skeletons in the closet?

"You see, we use clichés all the time but some days they hit the bullseye of our own emotional or physical state. Someday, every one of you will wake to find yourself staring in the mirror wondering if you have done anything good with your life, and your reflection will stare back smirking out the cliché that the proof is in the pudding,

AND YOU WILL WONDER WHAT THAT MEANS AND THINK THAT THERE IS NOT MORE THAN MEETS THE EYE AND YOU CAN'T DO ANYTHING, ESPECIALLY NOT TEACH THOSE WHO DON'T NEED YOU!"

The bell rang. Will Perkins readied the classroom for his next group of students and wrote the plan on the board, outwardly calm and methodical. His AP Language students had been given fertile ground for chat for the rest of the day. Some of them thought their teacher's outburst was just part of a good lesson, but others felt that there was something more, that they had glimpsed part of a raw interior and the experience was not pleasant. Others, of course, were merely amused. As for Will, himself, he was now gathering mental birch branches with which to scourge himself for losing his professional exterior in front of sixteen- and seventeen-year-old children. More than that he was obsessed with the events of twenty-five years before. Memories of then and of the phone call that morning crawled on him like snakes and spiders.

## CHAPTER 3

# PAYBACK IS

"Ah, come on, lieutenant, who else would drop a call out of nowhere? Who else do you owe, big time?"

Will knew the voice, saw the face in his mind, but more importantly, recognized the tone as the same one used with the gunner's mate and the others all those years ago, the same used with him also. It was the voice of the bully whose confidence alone made others weak around him. Could he hang up? No, you can't really hang up on your past.

"I can hear you breathing, lieutenant, and I can tell you know me. Remember I said I would cash in some time? Well, now's the time. Friday night at the bar around the corner from your house."

"Petty Officer Mote, I never go to that bar. And we have tickets for the ballet Friday night." He hitched his ancient robe closer around his penguin pajamas.

"Fine then, ten minutes before the performance outside the stalls' head. I got something for you to memorize."

Almost everyone in life is bullied at one point or other. While the berating, pushing, insulting bully is nerve-racking, the most insidious bullying comes from those who are alternately friend and bully, or those who are always friends on the exterior, but whose bullying is subtle and mean. Will's thoughts flew back to that night twenty-three years ago when the gunner took his life or so it was presumed. What must Mote and his circle have said or done to push the gunner to his death? Had Jervis, the big boatswain's mate, actually killed him? Did Mote direct some operation against the weasel gunner from afar? He was certainly capable of such planning as witnessed by his reaching into Perkins' consciousness and life to collect a debt after two decades.

Will imagined the slight, wavy-haired gunner landing in the warm waters of the Med that summer mid-watch. Did he watch contentedly as the ship sailed past, feeling the relief of separation from the others in Mote's crowd? Or, more likely, had he weighted himself so that he would sink traceless, and fall away from his nervous life and Mote into the dark, wet, warm womb of the sea? Will considered how happy suicide could be.

Their bedroom was large, but sparsely furnished with one large, peaceful painting of the lighthouse near Scarborough, Maine on the magnolia walls, a king-sized bed covered with an Amish quilt, two large bedside tables holding Victorian lamps and piles of books and cocoa cups, and an ancient sea chest that surprisingly matched their bespoke dark oak dressing table and high chest of drawers. The main feature was a rugged, oak bookcase that they'd found at the auction of a New England settler's house and held an eclectic collection from Louis L'Amour to Black's law books to a leather-bound *Beowulf*. Adjacent was a large walk-in closet crammed full of Beth's shoes and boxes of old college textbooks.

When he gave Beth her breakfast that morning, she knew he was upset, but then he was often upset in the mornings as he imagined some fresh challenge in his classes or had dreamed of some reckless student whom he could not control. When he was almost dressed and ready to go the school, his eyes were still diverted from her and she remembered that he'd answered the phone that morning.

Unusually, she turned down the broadcast from NPR (she'd

already heard the weather and chosen her outfit for the day), and sat up stiffly in her cream, cotton pajamas.

"Who was on the phone?" Her tone was one of concern and she looked at him as only a wife who's been married for twenty years can, searching for the signal or twitch or look that would tell her more than he wanted.

Pause. Will did not hide anything from Beth, but this was something he wanted to hide from himself, something slimy and unseemly that needed to be hidden.

"Remember SM3 Mote?"

Beth quickly filed through the sailors on the *Utica* and she could see and hear the stocky, cheeky, blue-eyed sailor in his immaculate uniform. He always called her Mrs. Lieutenant while grinning and even winking at her. Even when he was with his crowd, he would wander over to ask how she was and tell her what an unusual guy her husband was and how lucky he was to have such a jewel for a wife. She had been wary of him, but was also flattered.

"What? You're kidding. Why would he call you now?" Now she saw the look of Scrooge when Marley appears. This was some powerful ghost.

She drifted back to those halcyon days in Italy. Halcyon really was the right word, because it was the only real time of calm in her life. Afterwards came the drag of her climb to a law firm partnership. When Will joined the Navy and she went west to Berkeley Law, they drifted apart, even stopped writing. More than a year passed before that photograph came out of the blue. He'd heard from a mutual friend that there might still be a spark alive and he sent a beautiful picture of the sea taken from Taormina. She could practically recite parts of the letter written on the back of the photo:

*I understand how the romantic poets were inspired by an Italian ambience of wine and warmth, and the picture is beautiful but also empty. The sailor's life also has its own romance but both beauty and romance need an object. Is that you for me? It's possible. Like to come swim in the sea?*

She could not, or at least did not, refuse the offer of a beach holiday on the Tyrrhenian. At first she was coming with two friends, then with one, and finally she came on her own. He took her to his apartment in a sandstone villa overlooking the sea, where they drove the Amalfi Coast. They went to the movies on the ship together, their favorite being *Bugsy Malone*, much to the disgust of the crusty warrant officers. A year later, she finished law school and moved to Italy to study for the bar and drink wine, the newest on the ship with the title, "Navy wife – the toughest job in the Navy."

Like many young married couples, there was little separation between their dreams and reality. Of course, he would leave the Navy and find a career he loved; of course, she would pass the bar and find a good firm where she would progress to partner; of course, they would have a wonderful home; and of course, they would have two or three marvelous children. In fact, eventually all their dreams had been realized except the last.

"Yes. It was he on the phone. He'd looked me up and wanted to go out for a drink. I said 'no.'" While the words he spoke were even, almost monotonous, his fingers gave him away as he tried, unsuccessfully, for the third time, to knot his tie. Finally he gave up.

"Good. I would think he'd be in prison by now. I don't see why that should rattle you so much." After a couple of seconds, she saw her need to change tone. "Are you all right?"

"Too much for your legal mind, eh, counsellor? Well, I'm off to work. Let's go get some pasta tonight at that new Italian place."

Beth knew this evasion, and called it the 'distract her with temptation' ploy, but nevertheless was glad that Will was making a real attempt to put a brave face on his worries, and surprisingly even hiding something.

"Make a reservation for eight so I can wash some of the law off me first."

He looked at her and saw the last softness in her brown eyes before she put on her 'go to court' look. He envied her straight, shoulders-back posture, and the truth of her appearing at least five years younger than he slapped him. He had never told her of the last words Mote spoke to him on the ship. "Well, good luck, lieutenant. Remember, someday I'll need a favor and you owe me. Payback is a motherfucker."

They kissed good-bye and Will slipped into a reverie about clichés concerning evil.

## CHAPTER 4

# TALK IS CHEAP

"HEY, MR. PERKINS, WANT TO hear what I did in Palermo?" Mote was standing on the starboard wing of the signal bridge, which was just aft of the main or steering bridge, shining the brass on the flag locker. Junior officers were often addressed as Mr. rather than by their rank, so there was no slight or insult intended. They were on the 08 level, meaning eight decks above the main deck above the main deck, some 110 feet above the sea. It was one of those calm Mediterranean days when the sea looked absolutely flat aside from the ship's wake and there wasn't much wake since they were only making 12 knots. Since Mote's back was to the sun, Will saw more silhouette than features. Mote's blond hair and the red of his arms looked on fire on that warm, Mediterranean day with.

They were independent steaming (no other ships in company) back to Gaeta from the Balearics. There was really no reason for the signal bridge to be manned at all, since there were no ships to signal and any stray merchantman was miles away. Calm seas, sunny skies, and nothing really to do but shine the brass, of which there was plenty holding the flags in the port and starboard flag lockers.

The *Utica* had been a light cruiser in WWII, but in the early sixties, it was converted to a guided missile cruiser. It was a smart mixture of eras with an armored hull protecting four 600 psi boilers in spaces that had only recently had the old asbestos lagging removed from the pipes, and that also had two engine rooms, a central engineering control, and four propellors. It was a hot, isolated world down below, a world that was soon to disappear from Navy ships. Still, the old girl could throw up a rooster tail with all four boilers on line. From the main deck up, she had been remade into a more modern aluminum world, so now in the summer of 1979, she was nine decks high with flag bridge, bridge, and flying bridge looming above the sea. She was powerful with Talos two-stage missiles that could fly 120 miles, tartar surface to air missiles, anti-submarine rockets, torpedo tubes port and starboard, and (a remnant of her past) 5"/38 caliber guns port and starboard. Her combat information center (CIC) had the latest NTDS (Navy tactical data system). The Guinness Book of Records at the time listed her as the world's most powerful cruiser.

On the 08 level behind the bridge was the signal bridge where Lieutenant Perkins' CS division of signalmen plied their trade of semaphore, flag signals, and flashing light. Like boatswain's mates, theirs was a more ancient rating in the Navy and they saw themselves as real sailors, and not some modern perversion who stared at radar or computer screens.

"No, thanks, Petty Officer Mote." Will feared the usual scenario of disgusting alcoholic mixtures followed by a tale of sexual experimentation in a stairwell. He was determined not to be drawn in by the charismatic younger man.

Unfazed, Mote warmed to his tale. "No, really, you'll find this interesting. Ever read crime thrillers? Naw, I 'spose not, you bein' all educated." Mote moved closer to stand at Will's side, sunning his already sunburned and freckled face on the signal bridge wing next to the huge binoculars called "big eyes." "My buddy and I are writing a book about taking over a Navy ship. You know, kind of like Fletcher Christian and a modern mutiny, only nothing personal – just go for the money." Will found himself interested. Mote's allusion to *The*

*Mutiny on the Bounty* was an obvious ploy to draw Will in, but he smiled, happy to be hooked by something so intelligent and out of character.

"So, that presumes an awful lot," said Will, half looking at Mote and half at the horizon. "Can any of you write and do you presume that such a mutiny would work? It's not exactly sabers and muskets in the twentieth century, is it?"

"See, now you're onto something. We know there's money on this ship and we think there're ways to really screw things up so much that we could slip down the brow and off to Hollywood. It's kind of vague so far, but I figure we can find the soft spots in this tin can."

Will winced at the words 'tin can' since that is an appellation normally used to describe destroyers, not cruisers. Mote, as usual, was doing a good job of holding his audience. "I'm not sure I'm with you. Sounds to me like you're planning a straightforward robbery, not the taking of a warship or capture of its captain."

Mote moved still closer to his division officer trying to force the officer to look at him. "Naw, we ain't stupid. You hold up the disbursing clerk and bam comes the master-at-arms, bam come the jarheads, and if bam the guns don't get you, Staff Sergeant Majewicz will either kill you in the brig or make you wish you were dead. Then you get court martialed and sent to Leavenworth with a bunch of grunts who've turned queer."

The *Utica* was one of the few ships with a brig and the skipper had the option of awarding the old punishment of three days bread and water. In charge was the notorious Staff Sergeant who bragged that he'd never had a prisoner he couldn't break. While usually disciplined and professional, he also knew how to terrorize someone in the middle of night and make him want to behave. He was one of the few men on the ship that everyone recognized and most feared.

Will stifled a laugh. "Well, I see you've reached the author's problem. Ideas and plots are cheap, but your characters need to know more than their creator."

"Huh?" Mote looked bewildered as he peered at the officer's

practiced, passive face. "Well, I guess you're right. Talk is cheap, but how do we get to know more and would that be any fun?"

Will was thinking that if nothing else, Mote's quest to learn about the ship would give him something to talk about besides whores and fights. Here was more comfortable ground for Will – plots and fantasy, with no connection to reality. "So, you're actually planning a mutiny, not writing a book?" he asked in a tone of good-humored sparring that Mote had not heard before. Will's guard was slipping and he felt the beginnings of a smile at the corners of his eyes.

Now Mote lowered his sword of belligerent sarcasm. Could the officer actually be talking to him like an equal or at least something approaching a human being? Should he back Perkins into a corner or pass a little time with a fantasy? "Oh, come on, lieutenant. Would I ever think about something as horrible as a mutiny? No, this is simple robbery and murder."

They both laughed and Will found himself leaning on the rail of the signal bridge two feet from Mote, his ball cap off letting the breeze blow through his cropped, brown hair.

"See, maybe it works like this," Mote continued, his broad hands now shaping his tale. "It's payday and these two guys rob the payroll and create enough murder and disaster on the ship that they can get off the brow without really being missed."

"Ah, so," answered Will, now allowing himself to smile, but not looking at Mote, "nothing really to do with the Navy or ships, but just a simple stick up with a diversion."

"Whadaya mean, a diversion? Isn't that something on a road?"

"Yes, well a road diversion takes one a different way to avoid road works or an accident. In this case, your diversion will divert or send the others on the ship a different way while you and your evil partner take the road to riches. And where does your road lead you? Back to that Swedish girl in Majorca?" For the first time in the more than two years he'd been on board, Will felt relaxed in a conversation with one of his men. His shoulders fell and he was ready to listen and embrace a sense of being sailors at sea together like a Conrad tale of men belonging on their ship home.

"Hey, maybe you should write this book, lieutenant. You got the vocabulary for it." Both of them were pleasantly smirking at Mote's parody of his usual baiting bullying of his division officer, because this time the banter seemed like just that – normal male berating of one another – not a threat, and devoid of any need to humiliate or build power. "We had some fun talking about the book, but then we got stuck." Mote was drumming his hands on the wooden bridge rail as if he were trying to find the right beat for a song. "We don't know enough."

"Don't know enough about writing? Don't know enough about thieving and killing?"

Mote squinted and glanced at Will to discern any threat and discovered a sense of humor in the stuck-up bastard that matched his own. He laughed easily and loudly, half feigned and half appreciative. "Naw, you know, we got thieving covered and murder is in my genes. We ain't really writing, just having fun. What we don't know is enough about the ship and how it works and how to plan and all that criminal mastermind stuff."

Will paused, not so long as to make Mote return to his usual thug's face, but long enough to reflect on an author's need for research and authenticity. "Ah, you face the drudgery of writing. Fun to tell the story and imagine getting the money, but a drag trying to learn the details that will flesh out your plot."

"Lost you there, lieutenant, but I guess you mean it's more fun to do than to think."

Mote and Will both understood that Mote had succinctly and intelligently expressed the salient difference between the two of them – the Ivy League introvert looking for solace in his own musings and the streetwise punk always acting rather than showing that he had any savvy beyond an instinctive ability to charm, bully, and lie. "Precisely," said Will sounding like an appreciative teacher when his troublesome student gets the answer right, "but the thing is, planning and learning are doing also, especially when you have a need to know, when the learning has an application, when the planning gets you where you want to go." The two of them were inches closer now and decibels quieter. To see the two of them together, one would think they were telling secrets or sharing a reminiscence of a swell time together, or even planning a bank robbery. "In the book, where do you wind up? I mean, what do you do with the money?"

Mote was now fully at play. "Well, we sure as hell don't go to no opera. We take the train to Amsterdam and do whatever we want in the city of sin."

More laughter, this time genuine and appreciate of Mote's self-parody. "That I'll believe," said Will, "and I like your characterization of one of the world's great cities as a den of iniquity. So, the problem at hand is how to find out enough to write the story. Let's start with this: what rate is your buddy?"

In spite of the professorial tone of the officer, Mote was hooked into a conversation that he was not leading. It was a novel and somewhat alarming experience for him. He could feel his guard rising and a sneer returning. "Boatswain's mate. Why?"

Will sensed the tension in Mote, but was enjoying the sun and the feeling of relaxation so much that he wanted to lower the temperature again and return to the boys' intimacy. "Well, all I was thinking is that maybe you shouldn't be talking to me, because I don't know what you need to know. Remember, I'm a paper pusher in a tie, and a ship driver. Not much of a killer. Ah, but a boatswain's mate. There you have your born mother-loving, friend-defending, throttle-all- comers kind of guy. What's he know about the ship?"

Mote sensed that Will was trying to keep him on an even keel. The feeling was strange but ingratiating. Here was this rich sonofabitch actually talking to him and trying to make him laugh. He did laugh. "You got that right. Deck apes are all momma's boys ready to rip out someone's guts. They don't know nothin' but paint, the bridge, in-port watches, deck crap."

"And you know about the bridge and watches and signals. So, what else do you need to know?"

"Ah, come on, Mr. Perkins, we need the stuff that makes a crime thriller. Like who's in the way of us getting the dough."

"Money? What're you talking about?"

"Jesus, man, uh, sir, where do they keep all that payday money and all the money from the ship's store?"

Will turned cold at such a direct question. He took a step away while he searched a way to extricate himself from what he felt could become an uncomfortable, even disturbing conversation. He wiped the sweat off his forehead, put his ball cap emblazoned with his officer's crest back on, and said in a flat voice, "Everything you need to know is on the mess decks."

Mote wanted to save his resource for another day. He moved away, making himself as small as possible. "Hey, not a bad idea, and you can tell us all about the wardroom and the officers' wives." Mote grinned and winked before going to the other bridge wing to chat with a boatswain's mate, a slow, violent creature named Jervis, whose hulk was known to many of the junior officers because he stood watch as petty officer of the watch (POOW). Part of his duties in that role was to instruct the messenger of the watch to wake up the next duty section. Jervis was known for taking on the task himself and making sure the oncoming officers were wide awake by yelling, shaking, and turning on any available light. He bordered on the insubordinate, but usually managed to play dumb and innocent when his chief berated him as a dickless idiot. Will wondered what his wake-up techniques were with the enlisted men. No doubt he ran a culture of terror in his berthing area.

Will went below to another of his duties, that as the CMS custodian. Crypto codes were changed daily and his safe contained all the cards, instructions and papers to effect the changes. For this purpose he had a vault, a walk-in safe that contained further safes including the two-man control one where the codes for a nuclear launch were kept. The vault was six feet square, and just forward of the quarterdeck on the starboard side. The huge door was usually closed and no one knew when he occupied his hideaway. It was a perfect job for Will, since he could literally and legitimately lock himself away and pore over the records that had to be meticulous. Today, however, he was distracted by the image of sailors in whispering groups planning to take over. In his fantasy world, he saw them in eighteenth century garb running past him in their scores with sabers raised, winking at him as they passed as a sign of his silent complicity. Overall, he rationalized, a pleasant diversion from the monotony of independent steaming. But he did not sleep well that night.

## CHAPTER 5

# THE ELEPHANT IN THE ROOM

"SO, WHAT IS *MACBETH* ABOUT?" Will asked his AP Language students. Sometimes he used literature they all knew to encourage them to approach subjects from a different angle, or to write from a thesis of their own discovery.

It was Tuesday, the day after Mote had called, and he had taken Beth to Al Forno, the new Italian restaurant near the Garden. One of those open plan restaurants where one can see the chef tossing pizza dough, it was busy for a Monday evening and Will enjoyed himself passing a few pleasantries in Italian with the waiter. The food had been good and the conversation had begun as usual with Beth, after checking her make-up and hair, beginning a tale of office politics. "Jarvis thinks he deserves all the cream cases, like this class action suit. He's so full of himself that he can't even recognize that only a woman can develop any kind of empathy with a group who feel gender-based discrimination. So, I turned to him and asked him point blank if their complaints were real. He just looked at me like I'd asked him when he stopped beating his wife – which he probably does, by the way – and he began to mumble and slur. The dumb bastard was so caught up with how much money he could make that he never even considered the legitimacy of their case, much less how he's going to deal with twenty women with their claws out." She had looked at Will, who was looking back, and saw that he was gazing at a picture of a sailing ship, nodding and grunting at the right times, but obviously AWOL. "So, I said to Jarvis, was it good for you last night? Was it just a one-night stand or shall we go for a quickie at lunch?"

"Uh, huh," murmured Will who was now staring at a painting of the Ponte Vecchio on the far wall.

Beth kicked him under the table with a quick, "I'm over here and no I didn't sleep with Jarvis."

In his shocked misery, Will muttered his apologies and recollected himself and the conversation enough to ask, "So, did you get the case?"

Beth paused just long enough to see if she was momentarily more interesting than the Ponte Vecchio or whatever ghost was inhabiting his psyche. "Yes and no. Smitty told us to work together. How am I supposed to work with a trained baboon? No, sorry, an untrained baboon, who's likely to be so crass and insensitive that any arbitrator, especially a woman, is going to bond with the complainants and cast us with the useless pricks who run that firm."

"Doesn't sound like a case you should be on," said Will, who saw the situation as a perfect one for running away. He marveled once again at Beth's ability always to fight when she saw injustice.

"Oh, every misogynist pig has his day, and these ones are going to pay for the best defense they can get. Don't worry, my ranting against injustice like some sixties hippy won't last any longer than the time it takes to finish this delicious carbonara."

Will was still fascinated by his beautiful wife who had created herself layer upon layer, at once the shy college girl who was attracted to someone equally shy and scared, and the professional tilting her head to one side, gazing out of hard brown eyes with just the right amount of make-up, and making defendants and even her colleagues squirm; at once the fit, gym-visiting, fast walking counsellor in high heels and tight skirts, and the soft lover who often cried after they'd made love. How, he wondered, had he managed to grow so little in comparison? He felt himself weaker, not stronger, as he grew older, and suddenly reflected that he was glad that Beth never turned lawyer on or against him. Probably she knew that he'd be too easy to crush. "So," he mused, "do you ever wish we'd had children?"

He was as surprised at the question as she was and began trying to retrace his thoughts to see what cavern it sprang from.

Beth was only momentarily shaken as her mouth dropped open slightly. She drummed her perfect red nails on the table and said, "So, is this what's been occupying your thoughts or have you come across a sure way to drag me out of the law office?"

"Not sure. Maybe your beauty made me think that all that practice making babies hasn't produced any." He winked.

She laughed and winked back at him through a blush. "Well, practice, practice, practice. But in answer to your question, this is not the look of a woman brooding. It's the look of a woman hatching plans and schemes, whose baby is work and who is happily, joyfully married to a saint."

*Saint*, thought Will. *Saint Sebastian, maybe, tied to a tree and shot at by arrows only to be rescued and then clubbed to death.*

"But you, husband, have spoken the truth in the question. You regret not having children." They were both tingling with the novelty of talking about something that had not raised its head in fifteen years, but often, when admiring a baby or hearing of someone's grandchild, they had both sensed that there was an elephant peering in the window, waiting to be the elephant in the room that someone finally talks about.

*Elephant in the room,* he was thinking – *another cliché to talk about with the kids.* He jerked back to the reality of Beth's statement. "Yes. No. Well, but I think you are happier without children and that makes me happy, too, but sometimes I look at one of my students, like this wonderful girl, Charlotte, who is in one of my AP classes and I wonder what it would be like to have such a fascinating child. Sometimes I think the same thing when I see you with your dad – I mean, it's great being husband to the law goddess, but how would it

31

be to actually produce the goddess? Wouldn't that make me some sort of god?

Beth's ability to project and become a different persona on the surface from what welled deep within was not confined to her law office or public situations. When they were first married such was not the case, and she was openly irritable and tearful about their failure to produce a child, but time and practice allowed her to secrete her feelings away into what she and Will referred to as her little safe. But the safe seemed to be creaking open and only with a hard suppression of a part of herself, accompanied by clasping her hands in her lap, could she say, "Well, goddesses can be temperamental and you like peace too much for a riotous two-year-old."

"Hmm, I forgot they don't come out fully grown. Maybe I'll reconsider." He had missed the unease within Beth, so lost was he in his own insecurities.

"So, what is *Macbeth* about? Not what happens or who does what to whom, but what are the ideas that drive the play? What is the glue that holds it all together?" *What is the glue that holds my own life together*, he was thinking. What role would he play in Shakespeare's lexicon? Polonius, the old fool, who gives glib and empty advice? Poor Tom in Lear, naked on the heath, hiding his identity? Mercutio, slowly driven mad by his own ramblings about Queen Mab? Or, more likely just some courtier with a few lines, none very memorable, who has one brief scene or maybe gets to die on stage.

Charlotte was developing confidence after her clever answer to the quick write about clichés. The pretty girl in the front row, who liked to lean forward and display her assets, chimed in, "Evil – it's all about witches and war and giving in to evil."

"Yeah, well, maybe," the lazy one who knew everything except how to complete his homework retorted. "But maybe it's just about politics – power – and what people will do to get power and to hang onto it. I think the principal read it."

Laughter, including from Will.

The straight A studious Charlotte, who rarely spoke voluntarily, held up her slight hand and looked to Mr. Perkins for validation.

"Yes, Charlotte, what are your thoughts?"

Barely audible and still looking only at her teacher, she began. "Is it about fate and whether we really have any control over our lives?" She waited for Will to hold up his hand to silence some chatter at the back of the class and nod for her to continue. "I mean, like our teacher last year said, the witches are like the three fates and they keep tempting Macbeth or scaring him later on, but do the predictions have to come true? Does he have a choice? It's almost like a religious argument. Like, what do you call it? Calvinism and predetermination."

His pride in Charlotte continued the rest of the day to the point where he bragged about her to Eileen, his colleague in the department. But her words began to haunt him almost as much as the phone call from Mote. What choice did he have? Would Mote's control over him rise up after twenty years? Did he have a choice or was this his destiny? If he could find the weird sisters, he would have gone to see what images they could produce to show him the signs of his own demise. Would they drag out a series of images of burning ships with sailors drowning in the last apparition? Fate certainly did seem to be tricking him and he cowered under its gaze.

What if that's all he was and was meant to be? Lines from "Prufrock" began to haunt him – no, not Prince Hamlet "an easy tool, Deferential ....... Almost, at times, the Fool." He laughed inwardly at the word 'tool.' Too much time with kids and their insult of 'tool' for the hopeless ones.

After almost four years in Italy (he'd extended in order to earn his engineering qualification), he left the Navy and Beth passed the bar and started working on Wall Street. That was a time when he spent hours walking the streets, enjoying the rabble and rumble of the city, and the feeling of firm ground. But the ground was not firm. He wanted to start a family. Beth was equally enthralled with the idea of a baby, but then conception did not come as easily as it does for princesses and teenage girls in the back seats of Chevys.

He suffered the indignity of having a sperm count test, and she was told that she needed to stop menstruation in order for some endometriosis to calm down to a point where the fallopian tubes were clear. After several months of putting on weight and feeling like a walking water bottle trudging through life without any feelings of joy, Beth stopped the medication. They were approaching a decision to live without children and he went back to a place where he was comfortable – college.

Two years later, he had earned a master's degree at Columbia Teachers' College; Beth found a firm in Boston she liked and he started teaching at a good high school where he still worked, never contemplating anything other than a vague vision of retiring to his room full of his college books. While he was certain that he had not found the perfect career, he was good at teaching, occasionally felt that he really touched the minds of his students, and had long ago given up on the ambitions of others for him. He was fond of Prufrock's image of measuring out one's life in coffee spoons. Not everyone, he rationalized, can realize a dream. Some of us must dare not disturb the universe. *Some of us should count our lucky stars and know that we have found a silver lining*, he mused, slipping once again into the cliché that he believed he had become.

# CHAPTER 6

## HUNGRY DOGS WILL EAT DIRTY PUDDING

THE NEXT DAY, WILL WALKED through the mess decks, a claustrophobic place, always crowded and reminiscent of a greasy spoon diner, only painted haze grey and much cleaner. Formica-covered tables stood port, starboard, and amidships. Tucked away in the port aft corner, Mote and Jervis were sitting either side of a slight gunner's mate, who seemed alternately frightened and flattered by the attention of these two notorious gut rats. Mote's appearance, as usual, was impeccable with shirt ironed, clean-shaven face, and crisp dungarees, a counterpoint to his paint-spattered friend who never looked quite shaved and whose blue shirt was permanently stained with sweat. He was large, six foot two, with a huge chest, but his ability to intimidate came mostly from his almost bald head and an ugly, sunburned, flat face that seemed to say, "I can hurt you." Their companion was slight, about five foot eight with dirty brown hair, Navy issue "Buddy Holly" glasses, face still showing the marks of teenage acne and long, skinny arms that led to dirty, chewed fingernails. Will could not imagine why Mote had singled out a gunner's mate and his curiosity was so obvious that Mote looked up, grinned, and winked at his division officer, who colored and moved a little too swiftly to get away from the enlisted men and his own speculations about what might be occurring.

Mote was leaning back easily, shoving around his shit on a shingle (corned beef gravy on toast, aka SOS) as he said to the gunner, "Well, Jervis here likes to play this game he calls 'Just imagine'; passes the time and exercises his weeny boatswain's mate brain. But, like I say, he gets stuck in his own limited brain and comes to me to get him unstuck. Ain't that so, bos?"

Jervis scowled at the gunner, turning sidewise to show him a mouthful of mashed potatoes. "Yeah," he spat out, "gets boring chippin' paint so I imagine weird things, mostly about girls but sometimes about gunner's mates." He smiled lasciviously and the gunner edged closer to Mote, looking more and more like a suspect caught between two corrupt cops.

Mote continued. "Now Jervis's latest game is called 'let's get rich.' He'd like you to play." Mote smiled. "We think you're the guy who's smart enough to help us out." The truth was that Mote and Jervis had scanned the gunner's mates to see if there were any who had a "bad boy" reputation or who were misfits in some other way. They were sadly disappointed. These gunner's mates were as bad as OSs (operations specialists), looking like a bunch of college kids who were in the Navy to avoid the draft during the Vietnam years. There were thousands of sailors in the late seventies who had originally joined as draft dodgers but who stayed for a second enlistment, either because they found they liked the Navy, or, more commonly, because they couldn't decide on anything else to do. Their gunner, they decided, was the best bet, not because he was smart, or corrupt, or strong, but because he was the opposite. He could be flattered and intimidated and finally forced into anything they wanted. Like most bullies, Mote could smell weakness and the gunner wreaked of insecurity.

The gunner was obviously flattered to be noticed and singled out. Usually if he was noticed at all, he was promptly forgotten, so the experience of being chosen for anything was practically novel to him. He wiggled his torso to face Mote as much as possible, "What do I know?"

"Well," whispered Mote, "the first thing is if you can be trusted. I mean, we're just fuckin' around but some khaki bastard could still find some shit to charge us with. Know what I mean?"

The gunner did not know, but the sense of being in league with two such notorious tough guys was enough to make him roll over and play lap dog. "Sure, them khakis is always lookin' for something."

"That's right, gunner, so from now on we will be real secret with this game and arrange secret meetings, mostly ashore, like a club. Okay?"

This was more than okay with the gunner. Barely twenty years old, he had the maturity of a fourteen-year-old and a desire to belong that overrode any sense of foreboding. He came from a small town in Colorado where his parents ran a small store that was almost as dirty as the gunner. He joined the Navy because the recruiter said nice things to him. "Yeah, sure, okay, but what am I doing?"

"Well, you're just answering questions for now and, you see, no one besides me knows the full story, not even Jervis, even though it's his game. Let's just say it's a kind of board game and the object is to get as much money as possible. You're one of the players who helps us get the prize. Okay?"

"Sure," a relaxed gunner said, glad to think that Mote was his friend, even if he didn't really know or understand what Mote wanted.

"So," Mote was saying, wide-eyed and innocent, "the gunner's mates issue the weapons to the petty officer of the watch. Who can get into the armory? You?"

"Yeah, it's my GQ station, but them guns is worthless 'cause you can't get no ammunition. Every round is accounted for and only the chiefs and officers can get at it." The gunner was now animated, ready to show how much he knew.

"Okay," said Mote, "but the ammo is still there. All we got to do is figure out how to get enough for the job. When's anyone get any ammo?"

"Watches, but that's just the same all the time and then for target practice. 'Course I could volunteer to change my watch station and help with the ammo. There are a couple of gunner's mates who know the combos to get at the bullets."

"So why are we talking to you, asswipe. Who's got what we want?" Jervis barged in, suddenly waking to the possibility of having something to shoot.

For once the gunner was not intimidated, feeling he could contribute – to what he wasn't sure, but he also didn't really care. "I can do it. Just give me two weeks. The lieutenant and chief both think I do a great job, so they'll think I just want to know more about the rate."

"Yeah, they'd be right, you want to be a gunner, and I mean gunner. Get it, fart breath?"

Mote glared at his ape-like friend. "You're breaking the rules, Jervis. Remember the winner has to gain friends to get the prize."

"I got it," said the gunner's mate already looking bolder and bigger, buoyed by Jervis' vile strength. "So, I getcha guns and ammo, and then you go to the next stop in the game. What comes next?"

"Oh, it's just a game we make up as we go along. Meet us at Rosie's, and we can play the game over some beers. Jervis's treat," smirked the signalman.

"Sounds great," smiled the gunner looking back and forth at his two fellow gamesters and more than happy to be invited along to one of the shadiest bars in Gaeta.

"Yeah," said Jervis, his big, dark eyebrows raised in anticipation, putting on his softest voice as if he were speaking to small child, "it sounds real fun, huh?"

The gunner's mate looked hard at Mote and then at Jervis as his natural suspicious nature returned. "This is nuts. You're actually thinking about doing this. Get me out of here," he said trying to wriggle past Mote.

"Listen, gunner, we're just foolin' around, passin' the time, but it's more fun to pretend we're actually a gang. See? It's just play, but . . .," Mote turned to Jervis and smilingly nodded, "we can't let just anyone know what we're doing. Even talking like this can get us in deep kimchee. So, gunner, get the information, and then we'll start planning some more. It'll be fun as long as you only talk to us."

The gunner felt the sadistic hand of Jervis on his shoulder as he slid out. He could see 'LIGHTNING' tattooed on the big man's left fist and 'THUNDER' on the other. Even at half strength Jervis was hurting him and the gunner was reminded of that time he'd seen Jervis lash out full strength against that British sailor in Toulon, knocking him across the street and into unconsciousness with one vicious blow to the temple. "No sweat, guys, I'll keep you posted. Anything else?"

"Yeah, get to know some DKs."

Jervis and Mote watched the gunner shuffle forward toward the armory. Mote was drumming out a rhythm on the table as Jervis shoveled in some apple pie. Jervis stopped, looked at his blond friend, and wondered out loud, "Can we trust that pussy?"

"No, big guy, he's scared of his own bad breath." Jervis snorted, spewing pie down his stubbled chin. "But he's chicken. I been playing idiots like him a long time. Keep him scared, but make him feel special. He's like a dog – wants a master and no matter how much you beat him, he'll still be loyal 'cause that's the way dogs are made."

Jervis didn't really understand what his shorter, younger friend meant, but he was certain that Mote knew what he was doing. Like the gunner, he felt special to be with someone as smart and slick as Mote. Never did it occur to him that he too might be a puppet for Mote's entertainment.

## CHAPTER 7

# THE RETURN OF THE BAD PENNY

Whenever Will entered the Boston Opera House, he was reminded of the Duomo di San Gennaro in Naples. Both have a tall, central entrance with a striking carved arch, tall windows and a steeply slanted roof above, and both engendered in him a wonder about the imagination of the architect and the skill of the stonemasons. Inside, the theater was crowded, not only with the literati of Boston but also with ornate porticos and a homage to the past. The audience in their finery complemented this sense of the unreal with an array of styles, colorful ties, and children dressed to suit their fantasies and their parents'.

"Beth, you have become lovelier with age and what a perfect dress for you."

Beth turned to see a man of medium height with the girth to match his middle age and in a nicely tailored suit with a silk cravat, smiling from a tanned face through a blond beard.

"Thank you for the compliment, but I can't remember when we met," Beth lied. She was wearing a deceptively simple black dress, which struck an immediate chord with Mote as the staple of the smart Navy wife. This one was just knee length and beautifully fitted with a boat neckline and low cut back, complemented by a stunning pearl necklace purchased by Will in Majorca many years before.

In an instant, Mote knew he had an advantage. Liars always put themselves at a disadvantage. "No, of course not, my apologies. I'm Tim Mote, formerly SM3 aboard the *Utica*."

"Oh, uh, oh," stumbled Beth looking around for rescue by Will, a most unusual if not unique experience for her.

"Will is expecting me, but it really is fantastic to see you again. Of all the officers' wives, you're the one who treated us enlisted as something other than scum. Do you still have Edward, the teddy bear?"

What a remarkable memory, Beth thought, as she was transported back to sitting at the wooden table in a small alcove in a bar at Capodichino Airport twenty years before when two sailors asked if they could join her. They bought her drinks and were clearly in sailor mode until they realized she was an officer's wife, when their demeanor turned gentlemanly and they chatted happily about living in Gaeta and the eccentricities of the "old man". The two men had turned quietly drunk, but Mote had become sentimental in his cups, ripped off his crow (the petty officer rating badge on his arm) and handed it to Beth. Later on she cut it to size and put it on her teddy bear, Edward, who was dressed as a sailor. Will must have told Mote the story of Edward's crow. "I'm afraid Edward is not very well. He's held together by his clothes, but he still wears your crow."

Rumbling in the back of Beth's mind were thoughts of Gaeta and how the advertised relaxed time in the sun was also the time of her goal setting. Goal one, of course, was to pass the bar, but goal two, a bit more nebulous but at least as important, was to project an image of herself as confident and competent. Mote had been invaluable to her for he made her feel that she was remarkable and not just another smart woman with no personality; she could joke, even flirt with him. Never had she imagined that she would know, much less enjoy, the company of a rough sailor like him. Another person important to her in those days was the admiral's wife, who saw Beth as someone who could be an ally when organizing important social events, and smart enough (and whose husband was junior enough) to steer clear of the politics of wives worried about their husbands getting promotions and favors.

Mote laughed, almost childishly, and then realized that Perkins was standing on his left looking bemused in his unremarkable tuxedo at the pleasantries passing between his torturer and his wife. "My goodness, lieutenant, how distinguished you're looking, with your temples greying. Your wife is as delightful as ever."

"Yes, she is," Will mumbled, feeling suddenly warm and uncomfortable in opera uniform. "Shall we move to somewhere a bit more private?"

"I'm on my way to the ladies. Thank you for reminding me of a special memory, Tim. Goodbye."

"And to you, ma'am," returned Mote, now reverting to the sailor addressing his division officer's wife, "a real pleasure." They smiled genuinely at one another before Beth stepped briskly away.

Mote led them to a corner out of the traffic, noisy enough so no one could really distinguish their words in the general hum of the crowd. "So, lieutenant. Not much time before the show. Here's the deal. I need you to be my alibi – keep me out of a bit of stormy weather, you see. Here's a transcript of our conversation on February eighth at the Old Court Bar. You will need to commit this to memory and be ready to swear the truth of it all. My lawyer will be in touch to prep you for your testimony. Don't worry. You know I cover my tracks."

Will took the envelope, looked meekly at Mote, and said nothing, but was clearly close to shaking.

"It'll be a piece of cake, just a little thank you from you to me, some settling of accounts, right?"

"Payback is a motherfucker," whispered Will surprised at his own bold honesty.

"Nah, lieutenant, this payback is simple, but I have known payback to be a motherfucker. You know I have." The more Will looked away the more Mote peered at him and the silence between them became louder. The sound system boomed out a call for people to get to their seats.

"Isn't there anyone else?"

"Not like you, lieutenant. Besides they already paid me back or went to the Philippines, which is payment enough for anybody. Or they never survived, like the gunner." Mote was grinning his wicked teenager grin. He knew this plan was working. "I'll be in touch. Enjoy the show."

Will watched Mote walk away deliberately and then turn to wave just as Beth rejoined her husband. To Will she seemed unflustered by the whole encounter or perhaps even flattered.

"A brief but odd encounter, my husband," said Beth, perusing Will's face trying to gauge the nature of his mood. He was clearly a bit shaken.

"Yes, something I can do to help Mote. Just a favor to an old shipmate."

"Nothing along the lines of sinking a ship, I hope." Her comment was more pointed than she had intended. Will told Beth many tales from the *Utica*, both during their time in Gaeta and later, but she knew that there was something hidden and something that caused her new husband to draw within himself. For someone who consciously kept parts of her life or at least her feelings hidden, Will's laconicism seemed natural.

"No, just keeping Mote afloat," returned Will, regaining his composure. He was thinking of yet another cliché – keep your friends close but your enemies closer.

*Cinderella* is a ballet for all ages with its camp, wicked stepsisters, the romance of the prince, and the delicate beauty of the eponymous heroine. Will was working hard to enjoy the cleverness of the staging and characters and the magic of the dance, but his thoughts were on the poor stepfather, who obviously loved his daughter, but was caught by life to pander to the ugly stepdaughters; and of the sad prince who finally found his love only to have her mysteriously disappear without a scent of her reality or even a name. *He will find her, of course,* he thought, *but what will I find? Is life too much for me to have any charge or control or must I dance to Mote's tune and hope that there is some ending other than tragedy?*

Sitting there in that surreality of a beautiful place with pretty girls in their Cinderella costumes and an audience full of color, scent, and 'bravos' made him feel like a voyeur of an unreal life. Real life was on the *Utica* and the past twenty-three years was but an intermission while he waited for the main character, the charismatic and evil Mote. Fairy tales teach us how to deal with fear and evil with goodness and the prince and princess prevailing, but the big bad wolf always returns for another telling of the tale and poisoned apples are everywhere.

## CHAPTER 8

# ALL YOU NEED IS LOVE

WILL WAS WRITING ON HIS blackboard more than an uncomfortable week after *Cinderella*. It had been a time of many long walks and even more searching looks and probes from Beth, and he was slipping into a melancholic self-absorption.

Beth's week had been equally out of kilter, partly because the class action suit had cast her into a role of explaining how women think, but especially because Will's ghosts were also haunting her. Hard questions that had no precedents in law posed themselves: had they been fooling themselves about not wanting children? Had she been silly in her pleasure at speaking with Mote then and now? Should she pry open Will's secrets? The insecurity of the wall flower was looming around the corner.

Will's was the only board left in the school that required chalk. He maintained that any other board did not smell like a school and he needed to be able to run his fingernails along the board to emphasize his points. Under the heading, AP LANG, he wrote: "Voice. Does your writing sound like you or seem like someone else wrote those words?" This was a plum of a class, the smartest, or at least the most academic students in the school, who got good grades and, even if they didn't care about learning, did want the grades and prestige of an advanced placement class. Partly to take the wind out of their arrogant sails, he called them APEs, short for Advanced Placement English students. The bell whined, the high shrill having replaced the traditional bell for some reason that Will cared not to know.

"Okay, APEs. Your quick write today is to create voice – let us hear the unique you." Instead of standing at the front of the class near his desk and in front of the neat rows, he was at the back of the class, by the poster defining metaphor that read 'Memories are gold dust.' He had returned to his usual teaching uniform; in fact, it was his dress uniform of super-shined black leather shoes, Brooks Brothers blue suit, blue shirt, and Winnie the Pooh tie with the characters on a blue background.

"Write in a way that no one can copy, that expresses your own cadence, your own lexicon; that means your own words, even slang, and your own way of using language, your own way of connecting sentences and ideas. Write from all parts of yourselves –mind, heart, and soul. The topic: 'The Most Important Part of Life.' Think of all the parts of your life – past, present, and future. To use a cliché, think outside the box. What must you do with your life? What must you have? What will make you happiest? What is, was, or will be most fulfilling? What is it in life that is or must be you?

"Rather than pull an example from those who live through writing or at least make their living through writing, your example comes from a fellow struggler – me. I want you just to listen as I read – no text on the smart board, no hand-out, just my voice."

*I am haunted by the cant phrases of cartoons and bad movies as I search for those few words that will crystalize my soul's essence. Where are the words that will turn the most ephemeral part of ourselves into a universal recognition? Where are the right words to tell myself of the most important part of life and ourselves? When the role of teacher is stripped away and I am left with a kernel of self or self-respect, of what does that kernel consist? What do I want? What must I have? Is it as simple as the* bad songs about love? Is love really all we need? What words do we need beyond that one – love?

As he read, he moved through the rows to the front of the class, where he stood erect, occasionally lifting his eyes to stare at the back wall, his speech clear and rhythmic as if he were reading poetry.

*Max Muller said that "A flower cannot blossom without sunshine, and a man cannot live without love." "Love is life. And if you miss love, you miss life." So said Leo Buscaglia, but what sort of love? Are there levels of love, different kinds of love, good and bad love, unconditional love? Yes, unconditional love. And, yes, I believe there is. If all the literature and testimonies of parents are to be believed there is one unconditional love and that is the love of parents for their children. Yes, I know that there are bad parents but is there, must there be some love still? I know now after twenty years of wonderful marriage and fifty years of thinking about love, that the greatest love I ever received was from my parents and especially from my mother. I know also that I feel a vacuum in my soul that cries out for a child to love.*

*What emotional hogwash, sighs my intellect. Parents desert their children, put them up for adoption, even sell them. Is this unconditional love?*

*You cannot disprove by exception, especially when in all those situations, the desertion may be an ultimate sacrifice driven by love. Balance against your cynicism all those syrupy stories of women falling in love with their children at the first suckle or hard men melting into tears at the first touch of a silky baby. Or children returning home to parents in their most desperate times, or the look on parents' faces at the first soccer goal, high school graduation, the first steps. Surely the tales of tearful reunions of parents with their children after decades of searching for one another, especially parents searching for their children, are not just apocryphal. Surely, my own father's despair about separation from his children from his first marriage is no sham. No, weighed against all those other loves – friends, lovers, wives, husbands, even the love of children for their parents, it is the most often cited as unconditional love and sparkling clear – this love of parent for child.*

*But now, intellectually, emotionally, soulfully, I have come to an understanding of love and it is one that is missing from my own life. I think back to the shine of my mother's eyes and the little smile at the corners of her lips when she looked at me and know that there is no similar sparkle in my eyes, no outward smile or sign of an inward fulfilment. Sometimes I feel a rising of pride in the efforts and insights of my students, but the elation is short-lived since I know that my praise and pride is going home to their parents, to the bosom of their families. There is an ache, a void that I paper over with work, and books, and intellect, but which occasionally burns through the paper like when some asshole asks me what is most important in life.*

The tension of the class broke into smiles, a few giggles, and one or two shattering laughs as Will satirized himself.

*Of all Shakespeare's sonnets, I am most moved by the lines in Sonnet ii:*
*How much more praise deserv'd thy beauty's use,*
*If thou couldst answer – "This fair child of mine*
*Shall sum my count, and make my old excuse, —"*
*Proving his beauty by succession thine!*

Will's voice was now stronger and tighter as he dared to make brief eye contact with his students reciting from memory.

*So, here I am, almost fifty, bereft of the grace of giving love unconditionally, realizing that what I call the most important atom of life is missing from my own life. Can the most important understanding lead to the most important action or do I slide contentedly, but empty at the core, into a quiet death? I would not be alone. There are many who live childless and who seem to truly triumph over any societal or psychological need for children. But I may not be made of such stuff. I may not be strong enough or independent enough or ambitious enough. I long. I want. I ache. What to do? Where is love?*

Pause. Will looked up after a minute-long second to see Charlotte weeping quietly and boys shifting, embarrassed and uncomfortable in their chairs, as we all do in those few seconds of life when a soul is open to us and its owner is desperately vulnerable. They began to write, and after the allotted ten minutes had gone by in spooky silence, turned in their papers, looked at the blackboard for their next assignment, and read books of their own choosing for the remainder of the period.

## CHAPTER 9

# RED SKY AT MORNING

THE BEAUTY OF LIFE AT sea without women was that life became simple. The old line about singling up all lines and singling up all men goes beyond the lurid notion of infidelity in faraway ports; it also resonates with the psychology of survival away from home and family. For career sailors, the ship is home and while the ship may cruise an entire ocean, Conrad was right to say that some sailors never travel more than a few miles from home. And it is a home where one can feel a part of the structure and not have to worry about the tiresome details of life or indeed make many decisions. There is no struggle for work or position in the hierarchy, for a world where everyone knows precisely who is senior and who is junior removes much competition. Everyone knows the same rules and everyone knows that only one man, the old man, the skipper, is in charge. The resistance to having women on ships was more than giving in to superstition about unlucky women, or misogyny or sexism; it was a sense of loss of a way of life, of a loss of simplicity. At sea, the only world is the ship and it is a simple, secure world of eat, work, sleep, and occasionally telling tales. It can also be a beautiful world on a day of fair winds and a following sea when men can look over a blue world and talk of "the real world" left behind in port, which truly assumes a fairytale quality since the only world at that point is haze grey and blue and male. It can also be a brutal world where rank becomes bullying and tensions between officers and enlisted become palpable.

But not on this day. Making twenty knots, the cruiser was independent steaming under a hot Mediterranean sun and all those who were lucky enough to work or go topside felt the mellowing effects of simply moving through the ocean with no object other than to travel from one place to another. Dolphins raced the ship and dove under the bow as if to say, *you're a clumsy great grey creature.* Will was due to go on watch on the bridge at 1145 but had come up to the signal bridge at 1000 just to enjoy the day and see his signalmen. Mote saw him come up the ladder from the 07 level and greeted him with a toothy and cheeky grin, "So, lieutenant, where are we going?" he asked cryptically and conspiratorially.

"Petty officer, you know as well as I that we sail for Piraeus." Will felt his eyes tighten as he forced himself into his role, position, and rank. He was in shipboard khakis with its long-sleeved shirt and shined black leather shoes. Mote had his blue cotton shirtsleeves rolled up and his boots shone brighter than his division officer's shoes. Both wore their *Utica* ball caps, Mote's with the insignia of a third class petty officer and Perkins' with the officer's crest.

"My, what good grammar you have, lieutenant. I thought we were talking more philosophical like. I mean where are we really going? What are we really doing? Or is this out here at sea the real world and all that crap on the beach just a dirty dream?" Mote grinned ambiguously at his division officer.

Perkins stood a few feet aft of Mote on the port side where he could see the signalman clearly and did not have to stare into the sun. He chose to read the petty officer's unusual reflections as nothing more than small talk. "I see the sun has made you poetic, but I know what you mean. We are loose from the bonds of the shore and living in the fresh, clean world of sea and sky and men. There is, however, a rub, a problem."

"What's that, lieutenant?"

"Well, this is no sailing vessel, so eventually we'll run out of fuel. And, in any case, we'll need some food."

"Yeah, and women," jeered Mote, hoping to make his division officer turn red.

"Well, I suppose there is some need for women," he answered, disappointing his would-be tormenter.

Mote was, in fact, glad to see how relaxed and human his superior had become. It was time to learn from him. "So, tell me, lieutenant, when we trade this perfect life for a shitty life ashore, and I go back to dreaming about becoming rich, what's the best way for me to plan my dreamy, diabolical plan?"

"Impressive vocabulary today, petty officer." Will stared dreamily at the dolphins for a minute, allowing himself the luxury of thought and of making Mote wait. "Well, I'd say that in order to plan, you have to have a plan," he said glibly and obtusely.

"Right. What's that mean?" Mote inched closer to his superior hoping to both ingratiate and intimidate.

"Well, you and the boatswain's mate have this idea of a way to get rich and you talk and scheme, but do you have a step by step written plan with times, dates, contingencies, communication, roles, responsibilities and objectives?"

"That sounds like work. You think every thing that ever happens is planned that carefully."

"No way. I'm sure your big friend has no plan at all when he knocks the shit out of people. But most things that lead to something other than an ephemeral satisfaction are planned carefully. Then if there is something unexpected, there is at least a protocol, a procedure, a professional mindset to offset the random. Take, for instance, our exercises at sea. There are OpPlans for many contingencies. The more immediate plans, like a mock war at sea, are very much fleshed out and complete, but the real contingency plans that guide us in case of real war are a bit more general, but still specific enough to send us on a right path."

Mote thought for a moment. "You mean when we're on exercise

and you give us stuff about what's going to happen, when and what to look for, and what to be ready for, you're reading from a plan?" His eyes grew narrower as he entered this new world of ideas that take months to conceive and do not spring fully grown from the head of Zeus, or Mote.

Will pressed his advantage. "Sorry, you thought I was able to see into the future. I'm so sorry to disappoint." The lieutenant laughed and the petty officer jerked his head back to harrumph at his division officer's playfulness.

"Can I see one of these plans, lieutenant?"

"Sure, there's one in the safe." Perkins moved into the signal shack and opened the small safe (one of twelve safe combinations he kept in his head), producing the OpPlan that gave the general plans for operation of the Sixth Fleet in the Med. Mote handled it as if he'd discovered a grail, looking carefully at the organization, especially the annexes and appendices. He skimmed the document for a full ten minutes, intrigued by his brush with something he had never seen or really conceived of and yet ruled his life.

"Damn, lieutenant, this gives frequencies and safe harbors and chains of command and even backup plans."

"That's a classified document, so put it back in the safe," grinned Perkins as he started to make his way along the port side to the bridge. "Study hard and you can cross rate to become an OS." He smiled back at the studious Mote. For once he'd had the last word and disrupted Mote's security.

"Hey, thanks, lieutenant." Mote sent his signalmen onto the wings, ostensibly to keep a closer look out, and started to make notes. Later, in his rack he began to write on a legal-size pad of yellow paper: "Objective: to obtain the cash payroll of the *USS Utica* and create sufficient confusion and danger on the ship that the perpetrators have ample time and opportunity to escape without notice." *Damn*, he was thinking, *this is getting more fun all the time.*

## CHAPTER 10

# NOBODY'S FOOL

THE PIER AT GAETA IS about three hundred yards long with a high sea wall protecting the single ship, the *Utica*, from the vagaries of the sea. The Sixth Fleet commander's flagship is homeported there away from the bustle of Naples in a quieter, prettier, and safer place where he has a mansion overlooking the sea and his ship dominates the bay. The pier is concrete and crumbling a little in places. Coming back late at night, the pier threw several obstacles in the way of drunken sailors: bits of concrete sticking up, bitts, bollards, and occasionally supplies strewn in their path, and the usual rats who strayed away from the feral cats of the town at night. One famous story on the ship was of the POOW, who so hated the rats that he unloaded his .45 into one late at night. He got two, or so say the cognoscenti of ship lore.

Eight bells rang for 1600 and the 1MC boomed out, "Liberty, liberty, liberty for sections one, two and three. Muster the section four damage control party on the fantail. Now, liberty." Mote and Jervis were already on their way to their respective berthing areas; after ten minutes they were together on the quarterdeck where Will was standing officer of the deck (OOD) so another officer could go home for his wife's birthday. Mote saluted snappily with a curt, almost British, "Request permission to go ashore, sir."

Lieutenant Perkins returned the salute, "Permission granted."

The signalman put up the hood on his black sweatshirt emblazoned with 'Oxford,' smiled, and after Jervis was similarly granted permission, turned around on the brow to Will to say, "Thanks, lieutenant. I'll bring you back a story, a nice juicy one."

The two of them strolled side by side down the pier causing anyone coming the other way to move to the side, but still remembering to salute any officers and move aside for chiefs and first classes. They passed the dirt colored and dirty pier security building and walked past two Carabinieri before turning left past the beach bar that catered to Americans and slanted right into the gut. In those days, this corner of Gaeta looked at first glance like any other Italian village street with three-story houses, brown and grey plastered dwellings with iron balconies staring over a cobbled street. The difference here was that every fifty yards or so was a door with a flashing bar sign over it and plastic ropes hanging down to conceal the darkness within. Jervis was dressed almost identically to Mote in jeans, white sneakers, and black sweatshirt. In contrast to Mote's ironic Oxford sweat, Jervis wore a Rolling Stones logo with the tongue hanging out in contempt of all around. They went into the first bar on the right that flashed out "ailors bar," the 'S' having been broken like the bottles in the street. They sat at the back at a wooden table with red plastic chairs. A short, blonde girl, wearing a mini skirt and a tank top sleazed up to them as they entered. "Buy a girl a drink, lovey," she said in an East End London accent. The girls who worked in the bars were there to entertain and get the sailors to drink more while they consumed gallons of drinks themselves, watered and juiced to the point where they did not get drunk. Most had answered advertisements promising a glamorous bar job at a seaside resort only to find themselves broke and fighting off horny sailors. Some, it must be said, were more willing than others to 'put out' for a little cash, but most found themselves shacked up in a tiny room with a hotplate and a bidet, a toilet and bathroom down the hall, and a boy from Missouri missing his mother and his angel girlfriend.

"No, thanks, poppet, it's days until payday" said Mote in his most practiced posh British accent.

"Fuck off, whore," was Jervis's more succinct distillation of the mood of the two. When the girl went to the next pilgrims, Jervis and Mote stayed at the table in the corner where a generation of sailors had left their initials in the wood. "Speaking of payday, Motee, when're we gonna rob the fuckin' ship. I want some real action like in, whadaya call it, Ammerville?"

"Amsterdam, deck ape, Amsterdam." Only Mote could speak to Jervis in such cool terms without the tanned, filthy-nailed boy from Pittsburgh showing how the tattooed girls on his inner forearms could dance as he flexed his muscles. Sometimes the girls stopped dancing and he smashed his right fist, the one with '*THUNDER*' tattooed on the back, the gut of the disrespecting and unsuspecting shipmate. "It's gonna take a while. We got to work slow and methodical, like real, smart criminals. We got to disappear and never be missed and that ain't fuckin' easy with them khaki bastards calling muster all the time and checking on us in our racks."

"We ain't really gonna do this, are we Motee? It's just fun working it out."

Mote could see that Jervis really wasn't sure of the outcome or purpose of their games. "Naw, we're just practicing for when we get out and there's easier targets than a fuckin' warship. It's kind of like beatin' off thinking about the best lay that's gonna happen soon."

Jervis didn't really understand what Mote was saying, but grunted happily anyway as he looked toward the door for DK2 Rosario. Mote and Jervis had chosen Rosario when they were in a more business-like mood than when they had chosen the weedy gunner. When their fantasy took them to the point of actually taking the money, the sum of their knowledge was that you went to the little half-door of supply on the starboad side aft of the mess decks, produced your ID card, and got enough cash for one helluva good weekend. But they didn't know anyone in supply for there were other petty officers in the division in charge of stores. Then Jervis had said, "Hey, what about that chink who's in charge during UNREP?" (underway replenishment, when a ship receives supplies at sea).

"Okay, Ape, what are you talking about?"

"That fuckin' chink who works aft during UNREP – cusses like a boatswain's mate. Big for a chink and tough-lookin'. Fuckin' Rosie or somethin' like that."

"Oh, shit, you're right," Mote had laughed with a mischievous grab at Jervis' balls. "Ever hear the story about him?"

"Nah, man," Jervis had returned, grabbing Mote's offending hand and practically breaking the fingers, "tell me a story, you mama."

"Goes like this. Rosario, that's his name, was on the beach with a bunch of other Filipinos talkin' in Tagalog – that's what he is, not no fuckin' chink – when some drunken asshole from Ops came up to him and said, 'Hey, this is the American Navy, why don't you speak English and not that fuckin' Guamanian.' So, Rosario jumps up and sticks his face in the OS's and shouts at him, 'Guamanian! Any dickhead can tell I ain't no fuckin' Guamanian.' The OS is not too smart, so he pushes Rosario and that's when like fuckin' lightning, I'm tellin' you, he pulls out one of those Filipino butterfly knives and hacks off this guy's motherfuckin' little finger."

Jervis had sat dumbfounded for a few seconds. "That true? Who got mast? Who got busted?"

"Don't know, but I'm pretty sure that Rosario would just as soon cut your fuckin' balls off as talk to us and he ain't scared of no motherfucker even a fine specimen of apehood like yourself."

The next day during the dog watch, the two of them had gone to supply to see if they could spot Rosario. It wasn't hard. He was standing, arms akimbo, watching a DK striking (learning the job) seaman at work. When Rosario had sensed he was being watched, he looked up at Mote and Jervis and said in a light Filipino accent, "Dere ain't no fuckin' paint in here, deck grinders. Go topside and play with your chisels."

Jervis had hackled and clenched his fists, but Mote interceded and said, "Petty Officer Rosario, right? Me and Jervis here has got a bet about how the money gets on the ship. How about we buy you a drink at the Sailor's at 1700 today and you can teach us?" Mote had looked his youngest and most vulnerable, practically fawning before the muscular DK.

"A drink. Payday was last week. You ain't got no money."

Mote produced a wad of twenties, won on a bet from the others in his division, that Jervis could lift a P-250 pump above his head.

Rosario had squinted and come closer. "Yeah, sure. I think you might have something for me – back bar so I don't get seen with no fuckin' gut rats, three drinks and ten percent of the bet." Rosario had perfect teeth and forced a fake smile at the two conspirators."

"See you then."

Whether the stories about his causing another sailor to miss a digit were true or not, Disbursing Clerk Second Class Manny Rosario was a man to be reckoned with. After the Second World War, Filipinos still had the opportunity to join the U.S. military and many enlisted in the Air Force and even more in the Navy. If they served honorably long enough, they could earn their pension and U.S. citizenship. Most of those in the Navy, especially in the early days, did not find themselves in the more technical rates; they were not electronics technicians, or radarmen, or even enginemen. No, they were concentrated in the service rates, which were stewards in the forties, but had changed to MS or mess management specialist by the seventies. As a DK, Rosario was something of a renegade in the Filipino confederacy; in fact, he went his own way in most matters, spending much of his time with the white or black sailors on board and only attending special Filipino events. He was well-respected and trusted in his division and received high marks on his evals. Immaculately dressed on board, he looked constantly for ways to improve himself or at least his position. Among the other sailors, he was simply regarded as someone not to fuck with.

Rosario arrived precisely at 1700 wearing black trousers and a blue shirt. He was about six feet tall and muscular with his black hair slicked down and a gold chain around his seventeen-inch neck.

He strode directly to Jervis and Mote to say, "How much is the bet?" Before either could answer, the prettiest of the British bar girls walked over and leaned forward toward Rosario so he could appreciate her 'company.' Rosario looked her straight in the eye instead, giving her a look that sent her away without a word being spoken.

"Two hundred," smiled Mote, leaning back and kicking Jervis under the table before the boatswain's mate's grunts turned into something intelligible.

"Fine, gib me my twenny and I'm yours, Mr. Signals."

Mote held out a twenty, determined what drink Rosario required, then signaled three Peronis to one of the girls and prepared himself to win over this tough Filipino. "Well, Jervis here says that the ship starts out with a load of lira and dollars and there's enough so the ship don't have to get no more. But I say, we get it every month and someone carries it onboard from a bank."

Rosario looked at Mote and saw immediately that he had the big boatswain's mate under his thumb so he looked at Jervis gleefully and sadistically. "Ah, you ain't gonna get drunk next port, bos, 'cause you gotta gib all your money to signals here. You not very good at math, I guess, 'cause a year's worth of cash is a whole lot of money. One month's worth is over a quarter million alone."

"I ain't lost yet," returned Jervis, clearly disturbed by someone standing up to him, knowing that he mustn't lose it or Mote would be pissed, "'cause you ain't said how the money gets onboard."

"Easy, I carry it. Mote's right on. We hab an arrangement with local banks to provide dollars and local monopoly money. I go get it with the disbursing officer."

"Bullshit, you'd get stuck for that kind of cash."

"They stick me, dey get shot by either me or da disbursing officer. We ain't advertising. We just walk along in civvies with a briefcase that no dumb fuck can tell is handcuffed to me."

"Yeah, okay then, how come you or the sheriff don't take it? Looks easy to me."

Mote decided to intercede at this point before the DK insulted

Jervis again and Jervis lost a few digits. Clearly the DK was not afraid of Mote's bodyguard.

"Okay, look Jervis," Mote said quietly and carefully, scanning Rosario's face to ensure he was touching no raw nerves, "First of all, the two of them would have to agree. Second, he's specially chosen as the most honest, trustworthy guy around. Third, they'd have to plan real careful to get away with it."

Rosario signaled the pretty girl to bring him his second drink. He peered at the cheap paintings of Rome and then at the two gut rats sitting with him. "Yeah, everbody, eben the local cops know all about da money transfer and den I put it right in the safe when I come on board."

"But maybe," leaned in Mote, warming to the challenge and planning the verbiage for his OpPlan, "someone smart enough could get that case before it got into the safe. Maybe if there was enough crap going down on the ship, you might get to the safe a little late and a little short of cash."

Rosario smiled at Mote, clearly enjoying the fantasy. "Maybe you got more balls than brains. What crap is going on so no one's gonna miss dat kind of money?"

If anyone had seen Mote sitting in the dark with his big hands drumming on the table, they would have been correct in thinking that here was a man concentrating deeply. He sat back in his chair considering how much to tell Rosario as well as analyzing his plan for its effectiveness. Mote let the girl bring more drinks and the Carabinieri conduct their routine of checking the clientele who were leaving before he leaned towards Rosario, his back three quarters to Jervis. "All kinds of shit – fire so the DC teams have been called away, flood in the boiler room, and some even more serious shit. Enough scary crap so it would take a day or two even to get a complete muster, by which time the money and its happy inheritors are in Amsterdam smoking wacky tobacky and spending time with real women and not English drop outs."

"OOOOO," mocked Rosario, pouting his lips and leaning his

face close to Mote's and speaking in a heavier Philipino accent than usual, "you a serious mudderfucker. I bedder keep away from you or I get back to da Pilipines with nothin'. Next time I see da ship on fires when I got da the payroll, I know who to gib it to."

"Oh, you'll know in plenty of time, and you'll have a chance to review the master plan."

Rosario moved away, nudged Jervis, and said, "Da master plan by da master dreamer. I see you later. Bye, Jervis. You keep checkin' your back. Dis idiot likely to get you shot in the nuts." For the first time, Rosario smiled genuinely, drank his bottle of beer at one whack and strolled to the other side of the bar to join some sailors from supply.

"Is he gonna do it, Mote? Is he gonna help us?"

"No tellin', Ape. We gotta be patient and slow and organized and ruthless. Then maybe he'll be with us. But that guy ain't takin' no risks. He ain't goin' back to da 'Pilipines'." Jervis snorted while Mote reflected on the gleam of ambition in Rosario's eyes. Here was no angel. But here also was someone who took his chances if the odds were good enough. Time to cut out the risk and plan, plan, plan.

## CHAPTER 11

# MAKE YOUR BED AND YOU LIE IN IT

WILL THOUGHT OF THE BRAVE patriots whose actions were recorded on the plaques and walls of Boston as he strolled by the Charles looking at the Salt and Pepper Bridge. There was drizzle on this March day and he was cold in just his sports jacket. He could barely see through his large, tortoise shell glasses and his feet were wet because he was not avoiding the puddles. His mind wandered to the wonderful Cummings poem about spring and the world being 'puddle-wonderful.' Had his world ever been 'puddle-wonderful'? Yes, in sixth grade when surprisingly he made friends with the classroom bully, a blond boy named Slater, who took delight in pushing around anyone who tormented Will. The boy had looked up to a skinny, short Will because Will got As and helped him. Will always felt he got more out of their friendship than his strong, spitting friend.

But then came high school, especially band. Will played clarinet, which caused many unpleasant jibes about playing a girl's instrument and about sucking on long, hard things. His prime tormenter was a boy named Muller, who played first trumpet. He was famous for looking at Will during band, blowing kisses, and pointing at his crotch. When Will had to concentrate on the music, Muller would occasionally come behind him saying, "Oh, play the stick, lover boy, pretend it's a lovely, black cock. Make music. Ooooh, make music."

One day, Will said back to him, "Sticks and stones may break my bones but words will never harm me." It was a mistake. Muller increased his persecution and started bumping against Will in the hallways, mocking him by saying, "Sticks and stones, and long, black, slimy clarinets." He was afraid to go the restrooms, so he imposed on his teachers' patience and went during class time. He sneaked his lunch into the library where he was sure the formidable Miss Hucker would protect him.

Finally, Will had enough so during a trumpet solo, he moved behind Muller and pulled his chair out from beneath him. Backfire. Muller hit him three times and broke his front teeth and both of them were suspended, Will's only blot on a perfect record of behavior. Afterwards, Muller's name for Will spread and even his friends would occasionally call him 'the gay clarinetist.'

Will wondered if he'd always just avoided the bullies. On the surface, his time in the Navy and his current success as a teacher, not to mention his perfect marriage, would make him appear confident and strong. Today, perhaps most days, he did not feel strong and certainly not confident. Was he still having lunch in the library and going to the bathroom during class? Did he always avoid trouble? What hold did Mote still have over him? If he lied in court, there would probably be little chance that he'd be found out, and Mote would go away and leave him alone. Wouldn't that be good? Wasn't his life of avoidance a good one and hadn't staying away from the bullies worked so far? Besides, he did owe Mote who had protected him and without whom he would never be walking through puddles today. Then, there was the fact that he only needed protecting at all because of Mote. What if he told the truth? What would happen and could he bear to think of himself as someone who didn't pay his debts to shipmates? Mote would probably go to prison but not forever, and Mote's memory was long and his reach far enough to push a man overboard.

*No*, he thought, *I'm hardly the victim of bullying. More like the victim of my own penchant for avoiding trouble and confrontation. This is my own bed I'm lying in.* He was haunted by memories of random events, like the time he accidentally cut off a driver coming off a ramp on I-90. The other driver had sped up, pulled up in front of him so he had to stop, then ran out of his car looking like he would pummel a contrite Will. The pummeling was avoided by an abject apology by Will and probably a look of horror at his own thoughtlessness. Then there was the time he was lost in thought and walked into a bicycle. The young student just laughed and said he should daydream in a chair, not while he was walking. At unexpected moments, he would pull himself out of a reverie and imagine the consequences that might have been if the pretty, young woman on the bicycle had been pushed by him into the path of a car.

Beth, bless her, often reminded him of his courage of always trying to do the right thing, of standing up in faculty meetings to express himself, and of keeping good classroom management. *Not so brave*, thought Will, since he would hide after faculty meetings so no one could publically agree or disagree with him. As for classroom management, he had mostly good, caring students and he always spoke to his students in private, the recommended method of not humiliating a student, but also a way to keep any confrontation out of public view and a chance to back away from any real anger from a student.

And what of Beth? Was it really fair of him to lean on someone who had defeated so many demons without any real help from him? The image of her high school yearbook picture, one of very few photos of her (National Honor Society, choir, backstage crew) in the popularity race of the school annual, came to him and he remembered a story of her going to the high school prom with one of the popular boys. Turned out her lab partner had accepted her prom date only on condition that the popular boy would find a prom date for Beth. Her excitement, her practicing things to say, her dancing alone in her room, all led to nothing but a night of a few clipped greetings and an evening of smiling pleasantly while others laughed and enjoyed themselves. Needless to say, there were no after prom activities for her.

And what of Mote? Had he gone out on a limb for the sailor? Why did he not act when he found a hash pipe under Mote's rack during a berthing inspection – he threw it overboard and never mentioned and seldom thought of the 'right' consequences? Why? Avoiding confrontation or saving the one sailor he enjoyed talking and dreaming with?

What did he really know of Timothy Mote? Only what he was told, but there was one revealing tale from the signal bridge when the skipper had come to look through the big eyes and had a joke with Mote about the huge binoculars actually having a purpose other than scouting for girls on the pier. Mote had turned to Will and said with apparent honesty that he wished he had someone like the skipper in his life and not his old man truck driver whose interest in Mote seemed to end with his son's ability to fetch cigarettes and beer.

The image of scuttling claws on seafloors came back to him as he reached their brownstone and shifted to thinking about what to prepare for dinner.

# CHAPTER 12

## SWEPT ALONG LIKE A LOG IN A CURRENT

IT WAS ONE OF THOSE high cloud days that still felt sunny. Even though it was around eighty degrees, the brisk wind from the east and the low humidity made it seem quite cool. The signal bridge was directly behind the main bridge with flag lockers and halyards port and starboard for displaying the Navy and international flags to other ships, and signal lights port and starboard along with the huge binoculars (big eyes) and platforms where the sailors rose tall for semaphore. Connecting the two sides of the ship was a narrow compartment, known as the signal shack that contained lockers for publications, cleaning supplies (especially Brasso), foul weather gear and life jackets, sound-powered phones and MC (internal communications units), a safe, and most importantly, a coffee pot. There was room for one man at a time to pass the thirty feet through the shack.

Somewhat to the annoyance of the signalmen, Lieutenant Perkins had taken to sitting in the signal shack when he wasn't on watch and had a few minutes away from his other duties. Not only did they have to squeeze around him as they moved through the shack from one side of the ship to the other, but he had a way of asking questions and paying attention to their duties. Everyone performs better when watched, but the scrutiny was not comfortable for some. The empire of the signalmen was being invaded. SM1 Moody, the LPO (leading petty officer), was especially resentful since his regime of belittling his juniors was tamed and he even had to perform some tasks himself.

Perkins could sense their unease at his presence but knew also that his duty as their division officer did allow, even require, his presence there. That, however, was only a fraction of his pleasure at sitting on his metal stool on the 08 level. One could feel the motion of the ship much better up that high; more importantly, he was drawn to the fantasy of SM3 Mote and his wild plan to steal the ship's payroll. He had read the OpPlan and was scarily moved to consider the feasibility of this crazy idea – in fact, he was swept away by his own fantasy of how the plan would be executed. He put the OpPlan back behind the Allied Technical Pubs where Mote kept it with a big label on it, 'A novel belonging to SM3 Mote. Please do not read or remove.' The other signalmen would respect his wishes. He walked to the lee on the port side to watch the carrier ahead of them, since they were steaming as plane guard to the USS John F. Kennedy.

He was trying to analyze exactly why the reading of the OpPlan had excited him so; perhaps it was just the joy of reading a good 'novel' as Mote would have it, or perhaps just the cheeky brilliance of the plan, but no, he was into a realm of titillation he had not known. Perhaps it was a feeling of power, something he had never had. Others who assumed power lorded their superiority over him while he, retiring and quiet, found a place out of the way where he could escape to his books and fantasies. Perhaps, thought Will, he was coming to grips with the adrenalin rush of being an outlaw, or daring to break the most fundamental of rules of civilized behavior. The fantasy of being the highwayman was as refreshing as the breeze that day. The image in his head was of riding a wild, huge fir log down the Columbia River, of a man with a strength and nerve beyond his usual laconic soul.

"Did you read it?" Mote was on the signal bridge an hour before his watch. He had asked for the lieutenant's opinion and was looking for praise like a five-year-old who'd just tied his shoes for the first time looks for praise from his parents.

"Yeah," said Will not turning round, hoping that Mote could not sense that his division officer had been consumed by the younger man's fantasies.

"Well, whadaya think?"

Will turned slowly to look at Mote and felt himself drawn in, almost smothered, by the younger man's attention. Mote had become an alter ego to him, a bold persona that did not cringe at the thought of having to give helm orders loudly or force himself to stand up straight when he had to look at the captain squarely to report the events of the bridge. Mote and the plan were charismatic. "I think it's a good read. It could be a good novel."

"No, you know it's really an OpPlan. Will it work?"

"Well, I didn't really think of it that way," he lied, trying not to change color. "Let me think for a minute." Will knew what Mote wanted and had long been ready with an answer. "Well, I'd do two things. One is I'd get some eggs into another basket."

"What, did I describe a fucking Easter egg hunt?" Mote burst out, but then laughed.

Will laughed with Mote. "No, remember the old saying 'Don't put all your eggs in one basket'? Well, you need redundancies. You need to have contingency plans in case things go wrong or something can't be done. What if someone is hanging around when the fires are supposed to be lit? What then?"

"Brilliant. That's going to take some thought and another annex, but you're right. See, you have more of a criminal mind than you thought."

"You might also consider a way to communicate if there needs to be a delay."

"Delay, like what?"

"Well, what if liberty call is delayed or there's a recall or one of your main men is sick. You've got to have a way to communicate without arousing suspicion."

"Yeah, good, what else?"

"You need to give exact frame numbers for compartments, so no one goes port instead of starboard or something stupid like that. And, most important, you need to rehearse. No plan ever went off well without a rehearsal."

The idea struck Mote as especially dangerous and he felt himself change into his usual sneering face. "Yeah, right, we just blow things up and tell everyone we were just practicing."

Will wanted to retrieve the conversation. He said, in his best complimentary tone, "No, the brilliance of your plan is that you're the only one who knows all its parts," *except perhaps me*, he thought, "So you rehearse the parts. The boatswain's mate walks you through the fires; the OS walks you through the word to be passed on the quarterdeck; the BT walks you through the engineering spaces, etc., etc., until they know the plan in their sleep and they know exactly how a delay will be signaled and they know exactly what to do after they're off the ship."

Mote looked and smiled at his division officer. "That really how big operations work? Where do they practice a big military plan?"

"Well, for example, D-Day was practiced on the coasts of England."

"No shit. I might have to change my D-Day, but my *novel* is really going to be perfect."

The breeze stiffened as the ship listed to port during a course change to starboard. The two shipmates looked at the OOD on the starboard side peering through his binoculars. The normal world had turned surreal; a routine on a powerful cruiser seemed suddenly mundane and frivolous as they both imagined the wave of destruction and chaos they envisaged.

Will now felt nauseous. Here was the moment when he had to speak, when he needed to warn Mote off, when he had to be the officer. The wind was not brisk enough to keep the sweat from sticking his khakis to his chest and his scalp tingled. "Well, petty officer."

Mote bristled at the official tone.

"I was overcome by the excitement of the plan, and I wondered how much more excitement, even anticipation you might feel. You've put in so much work and seem to be wanting to put in more work, to make things perfect. But, you know," here Will could feel his throat closing, becoming almost emotional, and certainly quieter, "things have a way of taking over. Are you in charge or is the plan in charge of you? Time to, um, put it away and go onto something else." Will tried to assume an avuncular stare, but feared he just looked pathetic.

Smiling inwardly and putting on his best sincere, insincere face, Mote was inwardly smug at his intuitive understanding that Perkins could only go so far. "Not to worry, lieutenant. I know exactly what you're talking about. It's too big for me. It's over."

The wave of relief drew the tension out of Perkins' face, even though at some level he detected the disingenuousness of Mote's claim. He needed to believe the signalman; he needed to get himself off the hook. "Maybe there's something about the charms of Majorca in two days' time that will take you to a new plan."

"There you go, lieutenant, appealing to my evil nature. No, no plans for Majorca. 'Course them Swedish girls in Majorca may have plans for me." Young Swedish men in Majorca, free from the restrictive and expensive world of Scandinavia, were famous for drinking themselves comatose. Even American sailors admitted to being second rate to the Swedes when it came to drinking, but meanwhile, the Swedish girls were famous for embracing the attentions of sailors. They were back to their new normal - friendly but insincere. "How about you. Gonna go sailor on us?"

"No, petty officer, I've got shore patrol duty, and my wife is meeting the ship."

At this, Mote actually felt a pang of jealousy. He would love to walk around a beautiful port with a yellow SP band on the arm of his crackerjacks. He would also love to have the company of a pretty, intelligent woman, like Mrs. Perkins – a delight he enjoyed only in the occasional few minutes when he got to talk to her on the pier or in a port before her husband got off duty to join her. "Well, lieutenant, if I had a wife like yours, I wouldn't be the shit I am. Maybe that's why you're so good, huh? Wife keep you on the straight and narrow?"

"No, I'm afraid, she's more adventurous than I. I was born with a board up my back."

Mote didn't understand, but he did see that he was right to be jealous.

"Well, I don't guess I'll see her, 'cause she won't be hanging around in the gut, and I see you coming with your SP band, I'm running the other way."

Seven bells sounded. Time for both of them to go on watch. Mote grabbed the OpPlan and made a point of putting it in a burn bag as if the incinerator's jaws were waiting. He and his division officer both knew better. The tide was sweeping him away and all Will could do was hang on and plan his escape.

# CHAPTER 13

## TIME IS MONEY

Mote was sitting in his berthing area on the second deck (two floors down from the main deck) working on his OpPlan that he had retrieved from the burn bag and now kept locked up in the space below his rack (bunk). It was Sunday, April 8, and the rest of the division were out of the berthing area; the married men were on watch or on duty having traded with the single men so they could have time with family once the ship returned to Gaeta, and the rest were either on the beach or getting an early start in the gut. There was one small table crammed between the three high racks on either side and next to the head. On the Formica-topped table was neat, close writing on yellow tablets – pages labeled with Annex, Appendix, Glossary. Mote was starting on a new Annex K, communications, when he was awakened from his concentration by the gunner, "Hey, Mote, how's it going?"

Mote covered or turned face down his work as much as possible and turned sharply to the gunner. "This ain't your berthing area." In a second, he absorbed the tone of the gunner's voice, his greasy hair, his uniform shirt untucked, unshaven, grease under the nails of his skinny hands, and a look of a beaten dog crawling back to its master.

"Yeah, of course I know that," the gunner whined, "but I thought maybe we could talk about it." Mote double-checked that nothing could be read. He was in his pressed dungarees and a clean, white t-shirt. Unlike the gunner, he was clean-shaven and reeked of cheap aftershave. He decided to put on his kindly, big brother face. "Look, gunner, here's the deal. I talk when I want to talk. Besides I already figured out your role – you provide guns and grenades. You got the most important job of all, so I got to protect you. You see that, right?" Mote was smiling, leaning back in his chair and holding his hands out wide, face up in an attitude of welcome. "You see, you don't need to know nothin' more than that. I'll tell you when, the passwords, and when to get off the ship and our meeting place. I can't do this without you and the less you know the more we all are safe." *Besides,* he thought, *that way you can't fuck up.* Christ, he only has just a couple of things to do. Mote was angry but the gunner could not read his anger so Mote was sure he had the gunner under his influence, but he also knew that paper-thin egos are capable of nasty surprises so he had to stroke his co-conspirator and make him feel important.

The gunner stood back against the bulkhead, intimidated as usual, but enjoying the attention. "You'll go over it all with me sometime, I mean the parts I need to know?" Mote smiled the smile of an old friend. The gunner was forced into a broad grin. "That will be fun."

Mote stood and softened his voice as he encouraged the gunner toward the ladder. "Sure, we'll have beers a few times and work things through. You know we need to rehearse, too, so it's automatic, like finding the head in the dark."

"Great. That's great. I guess you'll let me know. Well, I'll see you around." The gunner started for the hatch and the ladder.

"Wait, you really want to help?" asked Mote in his most ingratiating tone, knowing his target would not, even could not, say 'no' to any request. He gave the gunner a crooked grin.

"Sure," with the edge of excitement. "What can I do?"

"Find me a BT who wants to play. Someone who really knows the engineering spaces." Mote looked directly at his prey.

On the spot, wanting to please but afraid to tell the truth, the gunner stuttered, "A boiler tech? Jesus, I don't know those guys. They're worse than Jervis. The only one I know is a guy from my hometown, but he's always in trouble and slammed me up against the bulkhead one time for asking if he'd heard anything from Farmington."

"Yeah, what's he in trouble for?" Mote was scanning his memory for a face he'd seen at captain's mast. He was in the habit of knowing who was in trouble since he felt a kinship to the troublemakers and they could often be useful.

The gunner could see in Mote's face that he might have stumbled upon a good answer and his voice came through more confidently; he even looked straight at the signalman. "Stealing. Even got busted back home for stealing cars. And he likes to fight. Damn good BT, though, so I heard some guys say one time."

"What's his name?"

"Anderson, David Anderson, BT2, used to be a BT1. Please don't tell him I mentioned him," pleaded the gunner, his neck and eyes reaching toward Mote.

"Hell, no, you guys never heard of one another, but I owe you another beer. Soon as we get off the ship." He grinned and gave a friendly nod, one of his more practiced weapons against those with weak confidence.

"Great, thanks, Mote. Anderson lives on the ship. I think he's restricted right now."

"Your country thanks you for your service," grinned Mote. The gunner positively skipped away in his excitement, while Mote shook his head and harrumphed.

Half an hour later Jervis arrived in the berthing area, saying he was on a smoke break from cleaning the port side bosun's locker. Once again he had extra duty, this time for calling his LPO a girl. He was sweating from his efforts and stripped down to his white t-shirt, or a t-shirt that was white when it was new. "How's the book coming? We any closer to gettin' into some action?"

"Patience is a virtue. Time waits for no man. Time is money." Mote's voice had changed from big brother to a parody of a preacher.

"Come on, Mote, don't fuck with me. What's goin' on?" Jervis was hot and not liking the work; he needed something to hang onto.

Mote looked at his big friend's face before determining that he needed to give the boatswain's mate as much as possible. He needed to make him feel involved and that everything was going according to plan. "Hey, it's goin' good, but this is a big deal that's got to be planned, rehearsed and executed perfectly." He looked to see if Jervis was cooling down. As usual his eloquence had cowed the big man into a quieter mood. "The plan is really going to shake this little world up, but we need a few more players. We need a snipe, we need BT2 Anderson."

Jervis' right fist 'THUNDER' involuntarily clenched in unison with his jaw. "What for? Them guys smell like grease and they think they're tough guys," Jervis said matter-of-factly, curious but more than a little perturbed.

"They are tough guys. That's one reason we need one. The other is that they know how to sink the ship." A big grin spread over the sailor's red face as he watched his big friend's fists unclench.

"Jesus, they can do that? But I thought we was just going to start fires."

"We are, but we need more. We need so much going on that we can get off the ship and not really be noticed and something that's going to take hours to fix. Something like the ship starting to sink."

"And a BT can do that? I thought they just shoveled coal or some shit."

"Well, this ship don't use coal. That's fuel that comes through those big hoses during UNREP, not coal. Be funny if it was coal, though."

"Yeah, then them BTs would smell even worse. You know this asshole?"

"No, but I think you do."

"Nope, only BT I ever talk to is that restricted guy who hangs out on the fantail and bums cigarettes. He's a mean sonofabitch."

"Yup. Anderson, David Anderson, I believe. When's he usually back there?"

"If he don't have watch around 1900, after chow."

"So, let's see him this evening." Mote's blond hair seemed to stand on end as he rubbed his hands across his face and head. "Couldn't be better. Let's go get our BT."

That evening Jervis lumbered up the ladder and out onto the port side with Mote right behind. The gunner was up on the five-inch 38 platform looking down at them; he gave a surreptitious wave that Jervis ignored and Mote acknowledged with a wink. Jervis spat to see how far he could loft the spit into the wind and Mote laughed at his juvenile, dangerous sidekick. It wasn't long before Anderson emerged from the hangar deck, spied Jervis, and immediately ambled forward. The sea was so calm that the ship was absolutely still, but even in port Anderson swaggered as he walked since his sea legs never really left him; even the dim evening light made him squint and look angry since he only went topside around this time of day and only then for a smoke. He was about six foot two, thirty years old, eyes that matched the haze grey of the ship, with balding, wispy, sandy hair atop a red, square jaw and a powerful 220-pound body. Even Jervis wouldn't want to mess with him. Anderson indicated to Jervis that he wanted a smoke by pressing two fingers of his right hand to his lips. Mote obliged. They smoked in silence and then Mote offered a second cigarette. "Thanks," said Anderson, "who're you?"

"Mote, SM3, friend of Jervis here."

"That's your name, deck ape? Jervis? Whatcha two doin' here? Look like you're waitin' for something."

Mote looked quickly into Anderson's mean, grey-eyed squint, measuring how best to proceed. Anderson was no dummy. He read people well and was like some kind of wild dog that could bite or run, but was unlikely to stay around to be petted. Anything subtle would piss him off, so would anything patronizing, and so would anything stupid. "We need some help from somebody who knows the engineering plant and isn't afraid of taking a risk or two."

Anderson looked at Mote for the first time. He'd decided that he was just another short sailor, some kind of rate that he didn't understand, that ran around topside and didn't really know shit, but he reconsidered when he saw something twinkle in Mote's eye, something like the look of a man who could get away with things."

"What you ever risk? What you know about trouble?"

Now Mote was on his back foot. The BT, as expected, started with a right hook designed to rock him and end the fight, and Mote knew he had to counter. "Well, the truth is, I avoid trouble. I'm lucky enough to find other people to get in trouble for me and I slip away. I hear you know more about the boilers and stuff than anyone aside from the warrants, and that you like to keep life a little interesting."

Anderson smoked and looked at the setting sun. *Yeah*, he was thinking, *I know more than most of those incompetents and that's what gets me into trouble, telling off the idiots who don't know shit from Shinola. I'd be a chief now if it wasn't for those idiots pissing me off.* He indicated he wanted a third cigarette, which Mote provided along with his *Utica* zippo lighter. Anderson glanced at the signalman quickly, lit his cigarette, drew deeply and exhaled, "Yeah, you one of them Teflon motherfuckers that laughs while others burn."

*Here was the critical point*, thought Mote. He indicated to Jervis on his right not to speak, by simply holding his right hand out parallel to the deck, as he surmised correctly that Jervis was about to defend his master. "Yeah, I guess so, but lots of people get away while other dumb bastards burn."

Looking at the big boatswain's mate who was holding his jaw shut and the little signalman trying not to smile, Anderson became interested. These two were up to something and he, Anderson, had nothin' to lose. "So, you're gonna get me off the ship and we're all gonna go run a whorehouse in Naples," he sneered.

"Close, except it's Amsterdam and I intend to have enough money not to have to work, even in a whorehouse."

Anderson leaned close over Mote as he ran his hands over his front pockets, cigarette dangling from his lips, and smirked at Jervis, who was trying not to gather his fingers into fists and Mote who was trying not to jerk or turn away. "Well, there ain't no money here. And there ain't no money trees on this fuckin' boat."

Time for a quick combination that would make the BT's eyes blink. "Yeah, there is, in supply, in a safe that's full of about half a million on paydays."

Without thought, the BT laughed and was on the verge of leaving, "You gonna rob the fuckin' ship and go to Amsterdam. You're fuckin' nuts."

Mote had to keep the conversation going. "Yup, wanna know how it works?"

BT2 Anderson squinted into the sun, flicked his cigarette into the sea and moved deliberately toward the ladder without a word.

Mote and Jervis looked at one another. Jervis broked the silence, "Well, I guess we're done. That fucker ain't coming to the party and he knows too much already."

Mote continued to think. *Maybe this rat just needs more reason to leave a sinking ship.*

## CHAPTER 14

# LOVE IS BLIND, HATE IS DEAF

THE NEXT DAY THEY WERE underway for Valencia, a short sail from Malaga for the warship and once again SM3 Mote knew he needed something or someone more than he had. He was leaning against the port railings watching seagulls. *How do you make someone do something that is against their nature? How do you entice someone to act against their better judgement or their own interest? What makes us leave our comfortable place? Either the place is no longer comfortable or there's a better place. Anderson was a born sailor. He didn't need or want anything beyond what a warship could offer. Women, money, glory, fame, adventure – nope, none of it and he wasn't afraid of anything or anyone.* He was so engrossed in his thoughts that he didn't notice that his division officer was standing next to him and he jumped at the sight of him.

"Christ almighty, lieutenant. Didn't your mother teacher not to sneak up on people?"

Will laughed at his sudden advantage over the younger man. "Well, I wasn't sneaking. Were you asleep or lost in some new nefarious adventure."

Mote decided to be as clear and blunt as possible. "How do you make somebody do something that's not in their nature or maybe do something that they really don't want to do?"

Now it was Will's turn to look at the sea and try to find an answer, but it was not an answer to the question as to why he felt he was always doing something he didn't want to do. He decided once again to take on the challenge of actually saying what he thought – of doing something that, on some levels at least, he didn't want to do. "Well, petty officer, my degree is not in psychology, but the answer to any question is to start with what you know."

Mote looked ready to wheel on his division officer and spat, "Goddamit, lieutenant, I'm serious. I'm trying like hell to figure something out and you just come out with some goddam grandmother's advice."

For once, Will did not wince against the signalman's angry frustration for he knew that the serious Mote was the man he liked best. "Well, goddamit, I'm sorry for your grandmother if she looks like me." He smiled and the muscles in Mote's jaw relaxed and his mind settled back from attack mode. "Okay, so this is what grandmother means. Ask the same question of yourself. What makes you do something you don't want to do?"

Mote considered. He was no Anderson, but maybe every fish is more or less the same. "Naw, you first, lieutenant. I gotta feeling you got a better answer."

Now it was Will's turn to feel the muscles in his jaw tighten. Right again, he was thinking. I am more likely to do something I don't like that he is. "There's a lot that motivates us. I'm thinking the strongest motivators are love and hate, or maybe money for some people, or probably fear for all of us."

After considering the list of love, hate, money, fear, Mote decided that only one applied to Anderson. "I'm thinking hate is the strongest thing in that list. Let's say we got a guy who don't care about love or money and don't scare easy. How far will he go if he hates something enough? You know anybody hates enough to go against their own best sense?"

"Personally, no, but there are plenty of people who will sacrifice their own lives just to get even with somebody, but they have to be really sick or hurt or crazy or maybe brainwashed."

Another good list, thought Mote. Anderson's not sick, or crazy and he doesn't have enough brain to wash, but he's full of hate. "Not you, lieutenant. You got big ideas and all that good stuff like love and honor and duty gets you going, but for us guttersnipes hate's the deal. Hates the thing that works for me."

The two men looked at one another momentarily without speaking. Each of them knew the import of their conversation was far beyond hypothesis. Will felt a bit afraid and sick at the thought that he had once again contributed, however unknowingly and unwillingly, to something he wanted no part of. Luckily, it was time for him to go on watch and Mote seemed happy to leave the conversation there.

*Getting closer,* thought Mote. *Anderson loves this ship and he loves being a boiler technician, but he hates the people who tell him what to do. Got to get that hate stronger than his love of the ship and his snipe life.*

After his watch, Mote was once again wandering the ship, looking and thinking. As he came out of the hatch by the port barbette, he looked aft and saw BT2 Anderson chipping paint – part of his extra duty punishment BTC Rodriguez, known for his creative and unique swearing, came up to the Anderson, let fly with a few expletives that would make most sailors smile with jealousy, and moved on. Anderson flipped the chief the bird as his superior walked away and began hitting the deck with venom. Pretty good hate there, thought Mote as he ducked back inside the skin of the ship before the BMC could spew forth at him or Anderson could see him.

Mote knew that his division officer habitually visited the signal bridge after his watch so after practicing his plan in his head he climbed topside to intercept him. "Excuse me, lieutenant," he said catching the tired Will between the bridge and signal bridge, "This'll sound strange but I got me a moral dilemma."

Will was too tired to argue, too tired to think. He had the midwatch that night and just needed some food and sleep. "What could possibly not wait until I've had some sleep?"

"Well, that's just it. We pull into port tomorrow and something bad could happen there, something that I could prevent, but it don't come natural for me to rat on somebody."

Somewhere between fantasy and pure bullshit, thought Will, but he knew that as Mote's division officer he had to listen. "So, what do you want from me?" he asked quietly, but almost insistently.

Without a doubt, Mote knew he was in charge, so he had no need to take unnecessary time. "I know somebody who's going UA as soon as we get in port. He's restricted so he'll make a run for it after restricted muster when there's people on watch who don't know him."

Either borne of tiredness or training, Will answered in an equally insistent voice. "So, why are you telling me? Tell the MAA, or are you afraid that someone will ask you too many questions?"

Mote smiled outwardly and laughed inwardly. He had prepared for exactly this response from the straight-laced officer. "Well, the MAA don't like me and you're the only officer or chief on this ship that I can trust – at least, the only one I want to trust. And I know lots of things that you don't wanna hear, things I know because people tell me things 'cause they know I hate khakis and they like to talk."

Closing his eyes as he leaned against the railing, Will breathed in and asked for details.

"BT2 Anderson, big, ugly, guy is going UA tonight." He waited and again got his anticipated response as his lieutenant opened his eyes, nodded and headed below.

The MPA (main propulsion assistant) and Will were hardly friends but they had a good, professional relationship. Will sought him out in the wardroom and luckily there was a place next to him. "Bill, I need to give you a heads up."

The MPA, a muscular, dark haired Acadamy graduate who married at Annapolis soon after commissioning, cocked an attentive ear.

"Scuttlebutt from one of my men says your man, BT2 Anderson, plans to go UA tonight after restricted man's muster."

"Not likely," the first lieutenant replied, "Anderson loves being a snipe too much to screw up that badly. You trust this sailor? Signalman, is he?"

Will looked sheepish, but he had to carry on. He could barely look at his fellow officer, as he softly replied. "He's a bit of a dickhead, disrespectful in a sneering sort of way, but I can't be sure he's lying."

His fellow officer's laughter cut Will, but he soon realized that the guffaws were not meant for him. "SM3 Mote, huh? I've stood watch with him. You can't tell. Slick little street-wise rat that one is. I'll let Chief Kettle know."

Will nodded tiredly and barely heard the gratitude in the voice of the first lieutenant.

That night both the MPA and BTC Kettle were standing on the fantail during restricted man's muster. The BMC was having fun suggesting that the chief MAA had the best collection of loose women in all of Valencia there for his personal pleasure, although his exact words were somewhat more colorful.

Kettle followed the big man down the ladder and made him move aside so the chief could go first. At the bottom of the ladder, the chief said, "You have a good time ashore then monkeydick. This man's Navy don't need no shit-for-brains pencil dicks like you, so go on and get your only-a-mother-could-love-it syphilis face outa this man's Navy." The chief sneered and turned his back on a seething, shaking Anderson.

The MPA went to the quarterdeck to alert them where the in-port OOD made sure his watch looked for Anderson during their rounds.

After two days in port, the SM3 had not seen Anderson so he asked his sidekick to find him. "Naw," said Jervis, "I already seen him on the messdecks. He stole two cigarettes and said the motherfuckers were out to get him. Pretty scary, that snipe."

Scary was not a word that Jervis used, so Mote figured his plan was working.

Back in homeport, Anderson finally showed up again for a smoke Reaching over to Jervis, Anderson grabbed the bosun's cigarettes from his pocket, took one, and put the pack back. Jervis stood still, his whole body rigid from being touched by the older, meaner man. The big snipe jumped into their conversation where he left it some days before. "What else I gotta do?"

Mote took it as a sign that it was time to hit the big guy with everything he had. *No risks, no grandeur*, he thought. I got this fish and it's time to land him. "We got someone inside who can get at the money. We get away because there's so much else going on, like gunfire, fires in the paint locker, and the ship's sinking."

"Ship don't sink unless there's water comin' in," the big snipe said unemotionally as if he were telling the time.

"Yup," and now Mote did risk a smile. "And I think you can make that happen."

Anderson looked almost friendly as he stared at the seagulls diving behind the ship. He leaned over the side to look at the saltwater discharges and laughed at the idea of the ship sinking itself. "Takes time and guys to turn all the right valves and turn off the right pumps."

It was sundown, and almost time for colors. "Come up to the signal bridge right after liberty call tomorrow and I'll go over the whole thing for you."

"You give me a hundred bucks so I can play poker and I know you ain't completely, fuckin' nuts," smirked Anderson, eyeing up the other two sailors who were tossing their cigarettes overboard. He looked around making sure none of his tormentors was nearby.

Without a word, Mote pulled four twenties from his wallet and indicated to Jervis to pull out his wallet. Mote snatched the wallet away, and pulled out another twenty.

"I'll be there. Then later," he continued in a voice that was less frustration and more a genuine plea, "maybe you can sneak me in some ouzo, but them khakis is watchin' so keep yer eyes peeled"

"You got it." Mote debated about offering his hand to shake and decided not to push it. Surprisingly, Jervis held out his hand and the two big men shook in silence, neither one smiling and both squeezing hard, measuring the other.

Unusually, the next day was a windy and wet one in Majorca, and the wet BT did not look in a mood for any humor when he arrived on the signal bridge at 1715. He had seen the BTC looking around the main deck and had to duck inside the skin of the ship to start his ascent to the part of the ship he barely knew. Mote signaled for Anderson to join him in the signals shack. "This is the plan," said Mote. You know Jervis and I are involved, but I don't want to tell you who else and I don't want to tell you all the other stuff that's going on 'cause that way you're as surprised as everyone else."

Anderson looked at the binder and the pages written in Mote's small, neat handwriting, and he looked around at the status boards and tactical pubs on the signal bridge. It was a world of the ship that he knew nothing about and he wanted to make sure he didn't get sucked into something. "What makes you think all this will work?"

Trying not to sound too glib or patronizing, Mote answered, "'Cause I got good people to help and I even got an officer to check the OpPlan."

"How many know about this?"

"Just six."

"Six plus the guys I get to help."

"Well, I was wondering if we could keep the numbers down there."

Slowly Anderson moved his big hands, staring at the deck as if he were closing and opening valves. "Well, take longer. Best to flood all the engineering spaces and that takes time. Got to be when the ship is cold iron so only the sounding and security and the cold iron watch are coming around every hour or so."

"Are you ever the cold iron watch?"

"Yeah, all the time, since I can't leave the ship anyway. And I can get any sounding and security asshole to let me do his duty. Yeah, I could do it. Can that big bastard help me? He don't know shit but I'll bet he could break some valves if I showed him how."

Now it was Mote's turn to think. "Give me a minute," he said, consulting his OpPlan.

1400 on a Friday before a three-day weekend when there's been early liberty. Number five has 50 minutes before . . .

1450 Number six causes another disruption TBD.

1500 number two lights fires in the port and starboard paint lockers and the hangar deck. Damage Control teams called away. Number five leaves the ship.

1515 Number three draws weapons and grenades and hands them to Number one. Number three leaves the ship.

1520 Number two leaves the ship. Grenade explosions in the port side gun barbette. Damage control team is now stretched thin and CDO will have to muster divisions to have any HTs and anyone else qualified make up second and third damage control teams.

1600 Number four comes on board with the payroll.

1630 Number one breaks into supply, takes money from safe. Bilges are filling with seawater. Sailors will be coming back to the ship to help. In the midst of the confusion, Number one leaves the ship with the money. The brow explodes behind him.

They meet the next day at 0700 on the road going up Tit Mountain except for number four who stays to testify that he never saw anyone take the money. Number four's money is left in Gaeta at a place of his choosing. Number six gets paid later and never leaves the ship.

"You could have him from 1400 to 1500."

"Not enough time."

"And you could have me from 1400 to 1515."

Again, Anderson turned imaginary valves. "Yup, that'll work if I get some valves turned before, turn off some pumps, and loosen the main valves." He then stared toward Gaeta and followed the line of the road to the medieval castle on the hill. "I never done nothin' like this before – just little shit, enough to always be in trouble. I ain't sure all this will work. But I'd sure as hell love to screw these bastards who think they know so much."

Mote knew that he had to project a confidence that would overcome the indecision of the cynical BT. Should he make a joke or get real serious? Another glance at the BT, who looked like some ancient behemoth who'd been transported to an unknown land. "All I do all day long is work through things that could go wrong. Then I ask my officer what else could go wrong. Then I fix it, and when we rehearse, we'll see what else could go wrong. I ain't saying it's a hundred percent, 'cause ain't nothin' a hundred percent, but it's as close to perfect as we can get and the winnings will make it worthwhile."

"You know somebody in Amsterdam?"

"Nope, but I know there's people there that need a good con man like me and a scary motherfucker like you."

Anderson glared at the signalman and clenched his fists. Smiling, he said, "Keep in mind that the scary motherfucker don't like little people who get him caught."

"Even more reason to make sure everything is perfect for our little adventure."

Anderson laughed and indicated he wanted a cigarette. Once more, he stared dreamily ashore while Mote continued to visualize the events of his OpPlan. He knew that still more diversion was needed, but he also knew that he had reached the point of no return.

## CHAPTER 15

# THE WISE MAN LISTENS BEFORE HE SPEAKS

THE CLEVEREST PHYSICS TEACHERS RELATE the principle of momentum to daily and life events. The force of the play-turned-plan-turned-OpOrder had taken over the lives of Mote and Jervis, who talked of little else. Mote continually pored over and modified his OpPlan, occasionally checking his ideas with his lieutenant, who made suggestions after sufficient reiterations that this planning was just a way to pass the time and learn more about the ship. In truth, he was consumed with the romance and danger of the plan. Mote, of course, said that nothing was being written anymore since the OpPlan had been destroyed and Perkins chose to believe him. The most important of Perkins' suggestions was to maintain security and to pay most attention to communications. His suggestions, in fact, did not make it into the OpPlan as code words that would indicate when a rehearsal was to take place and the day of the actual event. Rather, they were passed solely by word of mouth: 'Take a bath' to signal rehearsal day; and 'Wedding Night' for D-Day. The timing would have to depend not only on when they were in home port, but also whether or not the engineering plant had gone cold iron and the number of personnel on board. There were no dates written in the plan either. The rendezvous point, or perhaps town, for those who were actually leaving the ship (Rosario would stay on board) was to be part of the graffiti in Rosa's bar behind the toilet. As for other communications, Mote kept words to a minimum. Only he knew the entire plan; the others only knew their part, the passwords, and where to find the rendezvous information. They also knew the most important of all, which was the abort signal: "The fid has landed." (A fid is a tool, like a marlinspike, only it's used to untangle wire rope rather than manila. The word is often used to describe unpleasantness as in 'fid up the ass.') Will could only guess at all the details of the fantasy from his random conversations with the SM3.

During their most recent 'play' Mote had generally bragged that he could communicate with his brave few in code and really needed very little communication. Lieutenant Perkins had listened, half amused and half intrigued as usual, when he thought he might challenge the young petty officer by introducing some doubt. "You know, of course," he said in practically a superior tone, "that the best plans also pay attention to the communications capabilities of the enemy. And then there's the question of timing."

Their conversation resumed where they had left off when they returned to homeport. "Timing is easy," smirked Mote. "Not many on board. Right before payday with money on board but no one paid yet." He looked to see if his lieutenant was appreciating his cleverness only to find a blank face. *Got him*, he thought. Mote took a few seconds to determine if the lieutenant was actually saying anything else worthwhile or if he had become brave enough to fuck with his inferior. Nevertheless, he was enjoying their wordplay on the quarterdeck where he was standing POOW and his lieutenant, as command duty officer, was checking on the quarterdeck. They were just out of earshot of the inport OOD. "So, do I need to tell them how to communicate also?"

"Chances are that people who are standing watch, like us, already know how to communicate with the entire ship and the pier also."

"Yeah, but there will be so much going wrong that it'll be like cats on catnip in a hurricane."

"Nice simile, but maybe better 'deaf and blind cats on catnip in a hurricane.'"

Mote once again was surprised by his division officer's ability to think criminally. In his world, only those who actually carried out crimes thought of means to get around the rules. He had trouble understanding that the yoke of rule-following does not include a repression of fantasy. "So, maybe the lights need to go out and the phones need to die."

"That's what you think?"

"No, sir, that's what you think." Mote had won again as he saw his division officer's jaw tighten and his eyes seek out an image other than the mocking petty officer.

The next day Mote was thinking 'electrician's mate' as he scanned the pier through the big eyes. He knew he didn't want any more full partners, but maybe there was a way to bribe or force someone into disconnecting shore power and phones. He needed another thief and a good one, so he went to his radar in the persons of Jervis and Anderson. He knew they'd be near the fantail after lunch trading cigarettes and insults. When he saw them leaning against the bulkhead, both with arms crossed, they looked like two casual tourists enjoying the Italian sunshine and watching the evening promenade of local girls in their finery. "Buon giorno, dickheads," the signalman said, jerking his Neanderthal henchmen into life.

"Don't speak spic to me, you mouse turd," spat the lumbering boatswains mate.

"Well, spic normally refers to those whose language is Spanish. As someone fluent in the local tongue, I prefer wop or dago."

"Here's wop for you." The BT jumped to life taking a wild swing at Mote that both knew could easily be ducked.

"Okay, mi amici, I need a thief."

"Whatcha want us to steal, masterman?" misunderstood Jervis.

"No, no, listen, I need another guy for our little game, but I need someone who's on the wrong side of things – like a goddamn thief or murderer or BT or another flavor of scumbag."

"Plenty signalmen on board," proffered the BT along with a cigarette.

"Signalmen know nothing. I need an EM and a crooked one at that."

Anderson searched his mind for a candidate. EMs, like most snipes, were generally honest and hardworking and not easily tempted. Of course, there were some who were needy. "Well, there's one that's a thief but he ain't crooked. He's a kinda good guy who does bad things for good reasons."

Mote puffed philosophically on his cigarette. He was learning to draw out the best of the worst in the big BT and was thinking that you should never ignore the ideas and ramblings of anyone. You never know when one of them will stumble over something useful. "You know, I'm supposed to fuck around with words and confuse the hell out of people, but I'm stumped big boy. Enlighten me."

"It's like this. Washington is a real good guy – honest, hardworking, and funny like a lot of niggers and he wants to take care of his momma and sisters more than anything – it's like some bad, fuckin' movie – and he don't make enough so he steals. Got caught, too, so now he's completely fucked up 'cause he got fines and restricted and he still wants the money but da man is watchin' the black boy."

"No use to us," said Jervis, barely paying attention.

"Wrong, paesan', the black gang man here has seen how the black man can be useful. He who needs is vulnerable."

The big BT blew appreciative smoke while his dimwitted new friend waited for further explanation."

"We tempt, we catch, we deal, we promise to pay and Washington turns out the lights and the phones."

The next morning, as the gunner was getting his third glass of bug juice (flavored water reputed to double as cleaning agent), Mote deftly picked his pocket and handed the bulging leather to the BT who said he knew where Washington would be. Right before

Washington came smiling down the passageway, Jervis dropped the wallet where Washington was bound to see it.

Within thirty minutes, Jervis watched as the EM smiled his way to the MAA shack to turn in the wallet minus the wad of dollars. Twenty minutes later, after Anderson had shown him the way, Mote made his way below the main deck to the spaces where the buss boards that receive shore power were located. The clang on the metal ladders shot through the maze of pipes and pumps and alerted Washington, who was standing next to the buss board where he kept watch on the shore power supply. Washington turned abruptly when he heard Mote on the steel grate. His usual smile left him as something in him made him recoil from the red-faced grin that came closer.

"How's your momma, Filbert?"

In spite of Mote's thick arms and obvious bellicosity, Washington lifted his nineteen-year-old five foot six to match Mote's five seven and looked the older man straight in the eyes. He was in neat, clean, engineering coveralls and his hair was Marine standard. "Don't nobody get to talk about my momma, but me. Who you?"

"Mote, Timothy Mote, SM3, the man who's gonna help you get even more money to your momma and sisters."

"I don't need no freckle face hepping me. I take care of my own family." Washington had gone into a kind of automatic response, but now he slumped a bit at the realization that this devil image in front of him had satanic powers to know Washington's predicament.

"Well, see, here's the deal. You ain't gonna help nobody when we tell the MAA where you got that money from 'cause you gonna get a free trip home or maybe via Leavenworth. You see your predicament?"

"How you. . ." started Washington before realizing that he'd been set up. No longer was he the appearance of the brave sailor, but rather a slumped teenager ready to cry for his young wife in their tiny apartment and for his family back in America.

Although he himself was unsure if he felt real sympathy or just the satisfaction of victory, Mote put his hand on Washington's shoulder. "See, you think I'm the devil and you're being sent to hell there, big man, but you're wrong. I'm a bad man and I like to help out good guys like you. You gonna come out of this with the money you took and two thousand dollars on top of that."

Washington withstood the discomfort of the blond-headed sailor's claw on his shoulder, and still looking down, hoping against hope, ventured to let some hope filter through. "What chou mean? What I gotta do?"

"I thought so. You're a smart kid. What 'chou' gotta do is keep your mouth shut. We never met. You don't know me. Got it?"

"Easy, but that ain't worth two thousand."

"Nope, but you got your mouth shut? Or did I just catch a thief? This here thief who been caught before?"

"I never saw you. I don't know you," pleaded Washington. "Long as I don't get into any more trouble."

"Well, trouble comes to those who aren't careful, 'specially when they holdin' a shit hand like you. What you gotta do is one day when I say 'take a shower' to you, you arrange for the ship's power and phones to get disconnected at 1530 on that day. But you're just pretending. A little bird told me you could make that happen, but can you make it look like an accident?"

"Piece of cake. Too easy. But you say I'm just pretendin'. How that worth two thousand bucks?"

Mote squeezed the EM's shoulder hard and stuck a fat finger in his face. "You not listening to me, little man. You not keepin' your mouth shut. I told you all you need to know and ever will know."

"Sorry, man," mumbled Washington. "Curiosity ain't gonna kill this cat."

"Right. Another day you gonna hear the words 'Wedding Night,' only this time you gonna turn out the lights for real. That same day you gonna find a letter with a little present for you and it's gonna look a lot like this." Mote released the younger man, reached into his pocket, produced a letter-sized envelope, and pulled five twenty dollar bills from it. "Down payment. Now tell me the passwords and what you're gonna do." Washington looked around and repeated the words.

"Good. Two more things. You turn off as much power and as much phone as you can. If someone says to you, 'The fid has landed,' you don't do it. Or you stop. And you make it all look like shit happened, nothin' to do with you. You gonna be the hero who fixes the broken you make. Now what's the words you're listening for?"

Washington had no idea what the words meant but he said, "The fid has landed."

"Good. Now tell me again everything you're gonna do."

Washington took his time, but finally looked into Mote's eyes that were too close for comfort. "You say 'Take a shower,' I pretend at 1450 to make an accident that cuts off phone and power. You say 'Wedding Night' and that day at 1450 the phones and juice go off. Later on, I find an envelope on my rack. I stop if someone says 'The fid has landed.'"

"Good. How long before they get back phones and power?"

"Thirty minutes easy. Got to rephase everything when it drops off completely like that."

Mote smiled. "Remember angels and devils have blond hair. Sometimes they the same person. But you don't know no devils. You don't know nothin'. You never seen me and we never spoke." He stared at the teenager in front of him, until Washington looked him in the eye. "Good luck to your family." Mote went away quietly and never looked back.

Washington stood still, checked the gauges that measured the power supplies, and mumbled, "Please, God, I just gotta hep my family. You gotta forgive me."

# CHAPTER 16

# LIKE IT WAS YESTERDAY

FOR MARCH 20, IT WAS unseasonably warm, having climbed into the seventies, so Will invited Beth to take a break since she would be working late that night, and to his surprise, she had accepted. The usual place, he had said, and that meant a certain bench facing the harbor from the northwest corner of Boston Common. The location was hardly an accident since that is where he had proposed marriage when he was on leave in 1977 and she said 'yes' before he got the words out as he was kneeling on the ground. Her precipitous response came mostly from wanting to leap at the chance, but also because she did not want the embarrassment of people watching them.

Will sat ready with coffee for Beth as he stared into a pink sky and counted the planes coming into or departing from Logan. He reached into his pocket and thought about finding a ring in his hand twenty-three years before, but this time he found the note from Mote. He let it go just as he saw Beth crossing the common. She had her lawyer walk going, long strides with face forward. Tired of wearing the dark colors of winter, she had chosen beige trousers and a high-necked pink silk blouse. As befitted her position and the day, her matching shoes were practical and low healed, and her open coat was camel colored, tight fitting, and knee length. *If she was not my wife,*

Will thought, *would I find her just as attractive and alluring — more, because she would be a mystery woman.*

"You look shocked to see me," she laughed and kissed him briefly but solidly.

"Oh, yeah, found something dirty in my pocket," he explained, glancing up at yet another plane.

After exchanging the usual pleasantries about their respective days – Will discovering some plagiarism by one of his younger students and Beth beginning to take charge in her class action suit – Will blurted out, "Remember Sperlogna?"

Of course, Beth remembered Sperlogna – it was unforgettable – but she allowed herself a few seconds with her eyes closed visualizing the white-washed village a few miles north of Gaeta that sat on top of a hill above the Tyrrhenian Sea. The streets, if that's the right word, were barely four feet wide and wandered, maze-like, to the top of the cliff. At the top, one could look down the coast at the Norman towers and be transported to the Middle Ages. Or one could imagine a mamma losing her child in the labyrinth and finding her hiding as a joke, while her mother berated her and called for the sympathy of her neighbors. "Yes, of course. Is this a geography quiz or has a memory made its way into your distracted senses?"

Will smiled. How was he to avoid a keen legal mind coupled with the sixth and seventh senses of his wife? "Something happened to us there, something from which we've never recovered, or more precisely, something we've never realized."

Now Beth had to search her memory banks. Was it the meal with the bad shellfish? No, that had been extremely unpleasant but certainly recoverable. Couldn't be the beautiful girl in the flimsy floral dress and high heels that Will hadn't been able to jerk his eyes away from. How about the time that crazy John, the lieutenant from Weps, had scraped his car through the traffic taking chrome and rear view mirrors with them, believing that doing so was the only way to get past on the crowded roads at Sperlogna Mare down the hill and up the coast. No, it must be some conversation they'd had. Something she had forgotten?"

"No pings from your memory sonar?" Will prodded, half in jest and half in frustration. "We were looking down over the Madonna statue watching the cigarette-running black power boats. A woman with a beautiful baby dressed like a starfish, as you put it, barely able to move in its thick clothing with legs and arms stretched out at sharp angles."

"Well, I can visualize the scene," said Beth with a feeling in her gut not far from the bad shellfish. "And I can hear your question. You asked, 'How about it? Shall we have a starfish?'"

"And you said, 'Yes, I'd love a starfish.'"

Beth's eyes glazed over and the events of the day faded as she floated back to their villa over the sea. Five families lived there, a married LCDR and wife below, the ship's MPA (main propulsion assistant) above, and the old man with his wife Tatiana, both in their eighties, and one of their sons with two obnoxious boys, Rocco and Gino. The entire building inside and out was tiled, mostly in blues. They were very scientific about their lovemaking, which made it more, not less, exciting, but when they left Gaeta there was still no pregnancy. She leaned closer to Will. "I guess we really never talked about it fully."

"No, not like us. We stopped talking after you couldn't stand the medicine that stopped your menstruation and you stopped taking it. The doctors suggested a series of tests and your career started to go into overdrive."

Beth considered Will's interpretation of the time. Best to state as clearly as possible her version of events. "Yes, there were other distractions, but I also think that we no longer lived in Gaeta, no more romance in Sperlogna, and we were tired of planning our passion around the possibility of a pregnancy and tired of dreaming. New dreams took over, I think. And I think that's why we never really talk about it. New dreams hide the old. Nobody remembers what they were going to do if their reality is a good one. Regrets haunt failure, not success." Beth thought she had said too much when she saw Will looking away toward the courthouse and the sky over Logan. Was she only speaking for herself?

Will jerked himself back to the moment to see Beth holding her coat tightly around her. Her face was not that of the lawyer, but of the young girl in the library at Brown whose look at him implored and asked. *I've hit a chord,* he thought.

The truth was that Beth was worried that she'd struck a nerve in Will, that he was feeling a sense of loss because he was not now happy. Hers was an analysis closer to the truth.

Will spoke first as the eastern sky darkened and the planes were more visible. "Do you remember what else we talked about that day?"

Did she dare risk humor? How far from himself was Will? Best to land the plane back on familiar banter. "Well, you know, I remember every word you've ever spoken to me. Late at night I write down your wisdom to preserve it for posterity."

Shocked momentarily, Will took a few seconds before he laughed. "Well, share those documents. I need them for class; but no, what I remember is that we talked about some sailors on the *Utica* and my worries about some of them."

Beth was back at full powers. "By sailors, you mean Mote."

"Yup, and how I felt that I should help him."

The vague and incomplete puzzle that had been trying to piece itself together in the back of Beth's mind was now beginning to frame itself and the pieces were coming together to form a picture. "Much like the way you need to help him now? I can see the picture, but I can't fill in the most important piece – does he have some hold over you?"

Will reached in his coat past Mote's note for his gloves, which he handed to Beth. He shoved his hands between his thighs. Saying the truth was hard, too hard, not only because he wanted to hide it from Beth, but also because he wasn't sure where the truth lay. "Do you remember the attack on the ship?"

"Oh, my God. Do you think Mote had something to do with that?"

"Never mind the details. What's important is that Mote was on my mind then when we started talking about having children and he's on my mind now."

"And you're thinking about children?"

"Yes." In a marriage where they shared everything, he mused, there were only two locked rooms. Maybe it was time to let loose both the thoughts of Mote and those about children.

They sat in silence, both now shivering from the gloom. Finally, as usual, Beth took her cue to say, "Just let me think. Talk to me?"

"Yes, I'll talk, but please don't ask me questions. I'm doing okay, but I need, or at least I want to work through all this by myself first.

Beth wanted to say something to the effect that marriage was there so people didn't have to work things out by themselves. But, on the other hand, Will had never made such a request before and he had thrown his shoulders back as he held her hands.

## CHAPTER 17

# KNOW YOUR PLACE

NOT LONG AFTER THE RECALLED events in Sperlogna, Will and Beth arranged a division party. All of them, bar a couple of seamen who were on duty, showed up at the beach below the Perkins' place, partly because of the novelty of the invitation, but also because that particular beach was rumored to be a nudist beach. They were like bees drawn to honey.

Will and Beth were following SM2 Dragila and his wife down the path that wandered over rocks and through scrub to the sea where a path led round the corner to a long, pristine beach barely littered for an Italian beach of the time with wide, firm sand, views of passing ships and the islands in the distance, and high cliffs beyond. It was secluded, peaceful, and starting to become noisy with sailors as they spotted two topless young Italian beauties heading up from the beach. The girls trooped by on the way up the cliff but they did not hide their assets and the division were already forming their tales of the best 'eyeglass' liberty in living memory. SM1 Moon's two boys, aged eight and six, had taken in the view with eyes and mouths wide open. They had inherited their father's appreciation for art and were soon laughing and punching one another gleefully.

Beth rarely went to the beach on her own, largely because of the sign scrawled in black paint on a decrepit board that said "Attentione Viperi." The two girls came past them with impassive faces while the two wives glared at their husbands, both of whom fought to look away to the sea. When Senora Dragila saw the sign, she stopped, screamed, and started to scramble up past Will and Beth. Beth turned after her and before they reached the top had put her hand on the younger woman's arm. "Paula," she said softly. "Aspet, per favore. I viperi non sono qui. Non visto e addesso sono troppo paesi." Paula's terror abated enough for her to hold onto Beth. It would be difficult to determine which one was more frightened.

Once on the beach, the party began in earnest. Paula had brought a basket of bread, cheese, olives, wine and salami, while the Perkinses provided cases of beer. Beth, dressed in shorts and a long tunic that covered her flowered bikini and the tops of her legs, also wore a *Utica* ball cap to keep the sun off her face. She soon discovered, once she found good damp sand for a sand castle, that most of the young sailors had never seen anyone build one before. In spite of her best attempts to get them to call her Beth and not Ma'am or Mrs. Perkins, she had failed. She found that they would take orders from her more than anyone else on the beach, so she organized them with buckets, spades and tiny Italian flags into a construction crew that was working on the walls of an eight feet diameter castle and moat. The two boys decided they were the nice lady's lieutenants and barked out orders or corrected the men in ways they thought would please their new boss.

Meanwhile, Mote had found a quiet moment with his division officer. He was not dressed as demurely as Mrs. Perkins, but wore a tight fitting red Speedo and his pale back was already burning. "So, lieutenant, a thousand thanks for your invitation. Grazie mille. For me it's a great rehearsal success party."

Will pretended not to hear or understand. He was almost trembling with the news and his fears of his complicity with Mote took on the specter of an end to his naval career and sure ruin. All he managed to mumble was, "Prego."

"So," Mote said quietly, squinting into the sun, "any big plans for Memorial Day?"

Will jerked back his head as he ran through the calendar in his head realizing that Monday, May 28 was Memorial Day, just two days before payday. "Uh, we're taking a couple of days in Rome."

"Oh, very romantic."

"And you, petty officer?"

Mote was loving a conversation that only they knew was about an entirely different kind of romance. "Just hanging around. You know, drinking and dreaming." Mote dove into the ocean, swam powerfully for a few minutes, and came out to join the sand castle building.

SM1 Moon had been watching. He put on his shirt and sidled his skinny body over to his lieutenant. "Sir, may I say somethin' to you? Kind of advice, really?"

Will suspected nothing, his LPO being entirely predictable – a reliable sailor, not too bright, but not prone to any kind of secrecy or subterfuge. Will guessed that Mrs. Moon was perfectly aware of her husband's peccadillos in other ports and surmised that even she took a certain pride in her husband's exploits as long as he didn't tell her and kept his nose, etc. clean while he was in home port. "Sure, shoot."

"Well, see sir, I seen a lot of young officers. There are those who can pull off a division party like this one 'cause you and your wife are a whole different class from us and nobody's likely to do anything really stupid. 'Course I'll kill 'em if they do."

"Well, uh, thank you, I guess."

"But there's one guy you can't trust and I think you know who that is. I seen Mote's before. He'll take advantage any way he can."

"Well, Petty Officer Moon, I don't think there's any problem here, is there?"

"Nay, kids, wives, bit of titty. Great party. But I seen you talking to him a lot and that's not good. Others seen it too. I ain't your chief, but a chief would tell you to remember that you're an officer and he's a slimy bastard. You can't get too close to him – got to respect your own rank, sir."

Will's worst fears were being realized as the skinny first class looked serious for the only time he could remember. "Thanks, petty officer, spoken like a chief. I guess sometimes every junior officer needs a chief to take care of him."

"Don't worry, sir. I can handle Mote."

"Okay. Thanks." Will sat apart against the cliff enjoying watching the sand castle's progress and Beth's obvious pleasure with the two boys.

The sand castle was completed, a full five feet high and its turrets topped with beer cans. Beth was taking a photograph and the drunken crew were congratulating themselves and being as polite and complimentary as possible to Beth. Mote was especially effusive in his praise.

That night, Will stayed up late sitting on the step watching the stars, or was he cursing his own stars?

## CHAPTER 18

# THE SHIT HITS THE FAN

FRIDAY, MAY 25, 1979, WAS the start of a three-day weekend. The ship had been underway for ten days for engineering trials and had pulled into port the day before. Some of the crew had gone 'to the beach' (ashore) the day before on a day's leave to extend the weekend to four days. Most of the others were also planning to get away for a break and the captain had put the crew into four sections with early liberty at 1200 so as many as possible could have a break. Of course, the flag spaces would be minimally manned.

SM3 Timothy Mote made sure none of his 'crew' had plans for the weekend; he had plans for them. He knew that his lieutenant would be going away so he would be out of the way and no one else on the crew was of any particular concern to him. Rosario would be going ashore later that day to replenish the cash so there would be plenty for next Wednesday's payday. Mote went to the pay window at supply to ask if he could cash a check. Rosario eyed him carefully and then said playfully, "Some poor bastard pay you for annuder sucker bet?"

Mote felt appreciated as he said, "Yeah, arm wrestling, dumbass thought I was weak 'cause I'm short." He handed over a check for $50. In the memo portion were the words 'Wedding Day.'

104

Rosario glanced at the check, handed over the $50 and said, "Got plans for da weekend?"

Mote was momentarily surprised at the big DK's coolness, but then said appreciatively, "Na, you?"

"No, maybe I'll go ashore. I owe a friend a favor."

At 0900 Mote passed Jervis who had gone for a quiet smoke with Anderson. He took a few drags on a cigarette before saying, "You guys seen the new bargirl at Maria's? I think I'm in love; must be my wedding day." The two big sailors managed not to look at him and said only "Congratulations."

Mote managed to find the gunner skulking on the mess decks, deliberately knocked into the nervous petty officer, and grinned, "Sorry didn't see you there. You dreamin' about your wedding day again, gunner?" That just left the electrician's mate. He would be in his work spaces where Mote handed him a ten dollar bill that he said he owed; the bill had two words scribbled on it. Mote apologized profusely and asked if he wanted a different bill, one that hadn't been written on. Washington made a lame joke about being glad it wasn't a one dollar bill since he didn't like someone scribbling on his, Washington's, face.

Mote and Jervis convinced their LPOs to give them liberty at 1000 on this Friday even though they had the weekend off. Mote wanted a few minutes quiet away from the ship. Those of his crew who had duty had traded or paid some other single sailor. No one would even look for them until Tuesday. Mote and Jervis followed their usual route along the cobblestones, beer bottles, and overhanging dying plants to the gut. Once in a dark bar obscured by the smell of beer, cheap perfume, and flashing neon, Jervis wanted to talk about the plan, but Mote was quiet, not answering as he surveyed the grime on the floor of the bar and the black eye of the bar girl. "Don't know what you're talkin' about, big guy. Let's just enjoy the sights of this delightful establishment and imagine that we're somewhere cleaner where the girls really are available and the barkeep speaks Dutch."

Jervis laughed. "Yeah, nice dream. Too bad we don't know no way to get to a place like that. Think the ship will take us there?"

Mote sat quietly sipping his beer for a full fifteen minutes going over the plan in his head one last time.

*Unusually, the ship had taken shore power and auxiliary steam from the pier in order to reduce the workforce needed. There would only be a sounding and security watch and a cold iron watch in those spaces. Anderson's advice had been invaluable more than once. He had instructed Mote in general terms about the nature of a steam plant. Of course, Mote knew that the ship used seawater for fire main and for toilets, but he hadn't realized that the cooling water for the big pumps, turbines, and feed tanks was also seawater. Although he later realized he should have known, he also didn't think that the fresh water on the ship was also produced by large evaporators; the most important role of the fresh water was not to provide drinking water or water for showers, but to feed the huge boilers distilled water. The constant water flowing out of the hull of the huge monster warship was seawater that had performed its duty. In short, bring in the seawater but then use it to fill the bilges instead of travel on its usual route and the ship would begin to fill up from within. Anderson was smart – he didn't really tell him anything so Mote could not only play dumb, but actually be ignorant, even misinformed.*

*Mote and Jervis had headed to the number one boiler room during rehearsal, but the big BT had stopped them at the top of the ladder with a curt, "You don't belong in here." They had only a brief look into the noise, steam, and clatter of the space, like looking into the heart of a huge, grey beast with its intestines bawling, heat rising, and a noise well beyond safe limits. Anderson screamed at Mote later on that any dickhead would know something was up if two deck apes were with him below decks. Late one night when Anderson knew which spaces were not manned, Mote and Jervis learned the locations of the valves they had to turn. Anderson would start the valve turning for them and close the overboard discharges and secure pumps before they ever arrived.*

Finally, Mote looked up at his big sidekick: "You know what? The ship IS going to take us there. Let's get back so we don't miss the boat." They strode, perhaps a bit too fast, back to the ship. They walked along the sea wall since many on the ship were just now leaving for a long liberty and were jostling around the bitts and bollards of the pier.

The 1MC boomed out early liberty at eight bells, 1200, "Liberty, liberty, liberty for sections two, three, and four. Muster the damage control team on the fantail."

At 1400, Mote and Jervis joined Anderson in the boiler room. With auxiliary steam coming from the shore and the boiler secured, the space now seemed dead and their feet echoed against the grates of the platforms. They went down one deck where they could look down on the boiler, down another to the boiler plate, and still further down well below the water line. Mote shivered as he looked toward the narrow, vertical ladder leading out of the emergency hatch three decks above. Not usually superstitious, he understood why the snipes did not like to be in this space alone, especially with the tales of the ghost that clattered up and down the emergency ladder. Anderson himself claimed to have seen the sailor in his 1940s uniform staring down at him. "Steam leak got the poor bastard," Anderson had said, knowing the horror of a leak of superheated steam that cannot be seen, but can shoot at temperatures and pressures that would cut a man in half.

Provided with cheater poles, like three-feet-long two-pronged forks, they clamped open the valves that let in seawater so tightly that two men would not be able to close them. The cheaters were then hidden in the bilges. Neither knew exactly what the effect of each turning would be. Anderson started to explain one smoke break, but Mote had put a hand on his shoulder and said, "Listen, my big snipe friend, you been good about only tellin' us what we need to know, so keep it that way. We don't know nothin' about what goes on below the main deck, never even been there and nobody is ever going to think different." Jervis had just shrugged, but Anderson had looked up and blown appreciative smoke over the side.

Shaking with excitement and fear, the three mutineers began to climb out of the space. Anderson opened the watertight door onto the second deck while Mote and Jervis waited at the top of the ladder barely breathing. Anderson looked back, gave a quick thumbs up, and Jervis leapt out right before a marine passed by on his way toward liberty. Jervis swung his huge head, mouth open, fore and aft before giving Mote the all clear. They traversed to the other three boiler rooms and the two engine rooms for the next valves, each space becoming easier and less nerve-racking than the previous one.

At 1440, Jervis left the after engine room ahead of the other two, scampered up one deck, and went onto the main deck on the port side. Nice breeze, he noticed, just right for lighting a fire. Very few sailors were on the port side since they would mainly use the starboard side on their way to the quarterdeck, so Jervis worried little about who saw him, but he did make sure that no one was around as he opened the bosun locker. He had been collecting fire material – rags, cardboard, oil, oil-based paint – for two weeks, keeping most neatly hidden, but that morning he had built his little 'campfire.' Just in case, just for fun, he had stolen a few Salem cigarettes from a clueless fireman in his division to use as the incendiary. Jervis never smoked menthol cigarettes, considering them something that women and blacks touched. He tossed his lighted Salem cigarette onto the pile of rags and waited for a flame to leap up before he peered out on deck, then casually left the space leaving the water tight door ajar to provide air.

"Hey, Jervis, thought you'd be drunk by now." It was his chief who saw him on the starboard side and knew that his big petty officer was planning on a three-day binge.

"Naw, chief, I'm waiting for my booze ticket—kid who thinks he can outdrink me," Jervis grunted, remembering past exploits where he'd drunk for hours for free while leaving a trail of sailors passed out behind him.

"Yeah, well, I'm sure that'll be no sweat for you. Get someone to look after your dumb ass."

"You got it, chief. Say hello to Mrs. Chief for me."

"Right, she's always glad to hear from you." The chief moved quickly to his liberty, Jervis thought 'close call,' and lit another Salem, this one destined for the starboard bosun locker.

At 1450, the ship lost shore power. This was not a serious blow since emergency lighting made access around the ship possible and the 1MC was still available, but it did make the routine a bit slower. The OOD, a young ensign not long out of the academy, had his report from engineering ready when the command duty officer, Lieutenant Perkins, came to the quarterdeck. "Engineering reports it's just that damn unreliable Italian power again. ETR no more than 30 minutes." No one on the ship was too surprised. This was an Italy where the water was turned off if it was too dry and the power went out if it was too wet and offices and stores closed for mysterious holidays or family events. A young EM3 came past them on the quarterdeck on his way to troubleshoot and restore power. Perkins was nervous. "Ensign, pay close attention to keeping the log perfectly."

Mote was last out of the aft engine room, and he hurried forward to the armory. It was time for him to meet the gunner. He moved forward to just aft of the port side barbette to a little used emergency hatch near the armory. He found the hatch easy to open and slid down the vertical ladder. That part of the ship was quiet and the emergency lighting blinked on and off in the after part of the cruiser.

Mote hammered on the hatch that led to the armory but there was no answer. *Come on, gunner,* he thought, *open the fucking door,* but the door did not open. *Chicken shit,* he thought, but no matter, the whole gun thing was mostly just cowboys and Indians. Anderson should be ashore by now and Jervis would follow in a few minutes. Washington would be hard at work correcting the accident he'd caused and the gunner had probably also gone ashore.

*I can do without him, but I need to make sure of that little weasel,* he thought. He was running aft down the main passageway of the ship past a few marines and sailors leaving on liberty when his thoughts of how to deal with the gunner (carrot or hammer?) were interrupted by yet another call for a damage control team. *This fire,* Mote thought, *won't be the last one today. No one's even worried yet.*

Perkins had been about to leave the quarterdeck when a deck seaman came running up shouting "Fire!"

"Location, seaman. Frame number?" shouted Will.

"Don't know. It's where the boatswain's mates keep their paint. Port side."

In the confusion, BT2 Anderson took his permission to go ashore for granted and headed toward freedom. Luckily, there was no one on the quarterdeck who knew him – not unusual on a ship with a 1200 man complement – so no one recognized him as a restricted man.

"Petty Officer, 1MC. Fire on the main deck, port side boatswain's locker," boomed Perkins. Immediately after the 1MC announcement, the damage control team would be running to the damage control locker just below the fire. Jervis, meanwhile, headed to his berthing area, grabbed his packed 'weekend' sea bag, changed clothes as fast as only a sailor used to having to get dressed in under a minute can, and headed, not for the quarterdeck, but aft through the main passageway. He took a quick look around before moving into the helo hangar, the repository of the usual boxes, trash, small equipment, and ceremonial chairs. This time, he was less subtle, having stored two gas cans at the bottom of the pile. He lit the newspaper fuse he'd created and escaped to the fantail.

"Fire, fire, fire in compartment 1 tack 100 tack 3 tack alpha, starboard boatswain's locker." *Too quick*, thought Jervis on his way forward and Mote on his way to the gunners' berthing spaces. The explosion in the helo deck barely shook the ship, but did roll the marines in the barracks just forward of the helo out of their racks.

*What the hell was that?* Perkins was thinking as he ran from the starboard side where he'd been monitoring the progress of the preparation of a second damage control party to the quarterdeck. Right as a marine came running with the news of the location of the explosion, Jervis slipped ashore. "Son of a bitch," Perkins said aloud, while the POOW announced this third fire and the flag watch officer appeared on the bridge expecting an instant report. "Wait one, sir," he addressed the LCDR wearing the badge of AFSOUTH indicating his flag status. "Petty officer, hand me the 1MC. Ensign, phone the XO and CO. Tell them we have three fires on the ship." Will was no longer thinking. The hours of conversation with Mote were driving his imagination and his actions with a clarity that later shocked him, but now he was cool, professional, breathing deeply and focused. "Muster all damage control qualified personnel on the fantail," he announced as calmly as he could before booming at the ensign, "Close that brow. No one leaves the ship. Send anyone coming aboard to the fantail."

The OOD's muttered "but" was silenced by Will's glare. "All duty officers report to the quarterdeck." Will then turned to the flag duty officer, but was interrupted by the OOD, who swallowed and then blurted, "The phones are dead."

Will inwardly swore at himself for advising Mote too well. "Messenger, run to the pier shack and I mean run. Tell them to contact the XO and CO and request they return to the ship – that we have three fires." The flag watch officer backed away. As a qualified surface sailor himself, he knew he was in the way. "Lieutenant, I'll be informing the admiral. Let me know when the fires are out." He left the bridge looking for a flag petty officer to send down the pier to contact the admiral.

The duty officers were showing up. Weps LtJG Schmidt arrived first. Perkins had been chatting with Schmidt about the Reformation earlier in the day and was amazed at his memory for details. He thought this history major out of Holy Cross would be the right man for a comprehensive and detailed log. "Schmidt, check the log and keep it like your PhD thesis. Help out on the quarterdeck where you can. Get someone to check all your spaces." Then Ops showed up and Will sent him to the fantail to take charge of a damage control party and to arrange a check of all ops spaces. He spied Supply coming down the ladder from officers' country and yelled at him, "Get to supply and don't let anyone in. Check your spaces."

The gunnery sergeant, the senior marine, came and stood at attention before Will. "Gunny, I want your men at the following spaces: supply, engineering, the armory, the quarterdeck, and patrolling the ship. Understood?"

"Aye, aye, sir. Armed?"

"To the teeth, Gunny."

The Gunnery Sergeant, a Vietnam vet, smiled, hoping for a little real Marine work.

That left engineering. Where is that warrant? CWO4 Romstedt, one scary, experienced sailor in his forties, the only man on the ship who called the skipper by his first name, came running up the ladder, "What the fuck, Will, I got three fires," he challenged, expecting the younger officer to grovel before him.

"Check your spaces, especially the bilges," Will said, emboldened by knowledge and fear.

"Goddamit, I got two watchstanders for that."

Will stepped toward the warrant, staring straight at him, "And you and this ship are going to be sorry motherfuckers if you don't get someone down in those spaces!"

CWO4 Romstedt paused for a microsecond, turned on his heels, and headed for the engineering spaces himself muttering, "Holy fuck, holy fuck, holy fuck!"

# CHAPTER 19

## PRACTICE MAKES PERFECT

As AN ENGLISH TEACHER, PERKINS' life was one long trudge of papers with in and out manila folders for each period, and his own notes about upcoming lessons. His greatest fear was losing a paper from one of these folders, so he checked his box in the teachers' lounge religiously every day before heading home to see if a student had turned in a paper that would find its way to his pigeonhole. The so-called lounge occasionally served as a meeting place or lunchroom for those teachers who did not munch their sandwiches while grading papers at their desks in their classrooms, but truly was more of a workroom with two copiers, a union notice board, an admin notice board with all the requisite posters about reporting suspected child abuse and opportunities for training. On one wall on an ancient wooden table stood the four-foot-high grid of teachers' boxes. Will could not see, but only feel into his box and he found the usual bulletin for the following day, a statement of accounts for after school activities, a newsletter from the union, and a plain envelope with Will Perkins written in a left-handed scrawl. The letters on the envelope seemed to crawl up his arm as the glimmer of recognition stole over Perkins. "How can he know where I work and how can he know how to leave me a note?"

As expected, the note was light-hearted but deadly serious:

> Mr. Perkins, I have completed my assignment and
> I would like to discuss the same with you at the
> offices of Porter and Goodall in the Prudential
> Center on March 27 at 4:00 p.m. My Guardian,
> one Peter Hepburn, LLD, will be in attendance. We
> look forward to seeing you,
>
> As always,
> Timothy Mote

Prior to the appointment, Will made arrangements to leave school right after his last class and take a taxi to the Prudential Center, a beautiful area underneath the tallest building in Boston that was usually associated with the good times of shopping and eating. Porter and Goodall was on the twentieth floor behind glass doors with the names of the partners in gold. The carpet was a deep red, designed, Will gathered, to make the clients feel special enough to line the pockets of the advocates. The hypocrisy of his nice navy blue Brooks Brothers suit with cream-colored shirt and floral tie choked him since he was too aware that only his wife's 'advocate's' salary afforded him this appearance of wealth that was important to him for this meeting.

The grey-haired receptionist showed him to Mr. Hepburn's office where Mote sat comfortably with a lawyer in his thirties in shirtsleeves rolled up to show powerful forearms. *Ah*, thought, Will, *money following money, law following law, football jock following football jock*. The room looked exactly as he expected – cherry wood desk, bookcase with Black's law, table for six with a mirror-shiny veneer, picture window looking out to the *USS Constitution*, and a smell of fresh polish. The lawyer, speaking in a voice that was a few notes higher than one would expect from such a blond Adonis, invited Will to sit at the table in the leather chair with arms, across from a smiling Mote. Mote reached out before Will sat down to offer his hand which his former division officer took a bit limply. He wore a high-necked, grey, heavy sweater and brown cords, looking like some sort of old-fashioned merchant sailor. Always in the right costume, thought Will.

"Would you like coffee?" asked Hepburn

"Yes, please, black."

"Myra, some coffee, black, for Mr. Perkins. Thank you," yelled the blond attorney, a little too loudly.

"Ah, still got some Navy habits, eh lieutenant?" smiled Mote. Perkins remained rigid in his chair.

"So, Mr. Perkins, my client, Timothy Mote, tells me that his arrest for armed robbery is a case of mistaken identity, that at the time of the crime he was drinking with you. Is that correct?"

Will was stunned at the directness of the question. "Uh, I didn't know what he was arrested for, only that he needed me to say where he was one evening." In fact, Mote had only ever talked or written about the alibi and what they were doing. The revelation that the crime was armed robbery shocked Will who discovered that his hands were sweating. He hid them on his knees under the table while he shifted to try to sit more upright in his chair. "I can't say if I was drinking with him without some knowledge of when we're talking about." He was surprised at the edge of annoyance in his voice, and he was afraid he was too much in impatient teacher mode.

The lawyer laughed. "Sorry, I tend to get to the point a little quick. Let's go back a bit. How do you know my client?"

Will glanced at Mote, who had slid back in his chair as if watching a good film. "We were shipmates aboard the *USS Utica* from the fall of 1977 to the spring of 1979."

"What do you mean by 'shipmates'?"

Will wondered if the lawyer was stupid or just following his training of beating every sentence or word to death until lawyers are certain of the meaning and the rest of the world sits either confused or apathetic. "We were both assigned to the *USS Utica*. I was his division officer, which means I was the officer in charge of the group of sailors who were signalmen. He was a petty officer in the division, meaning he had some supervisory responsibilities but there were several sailors senior to him in the division."

"Did you see him daily? How well did you know him?"

"When we were at sea, I would see him most days, and in port I would see him every day at least briefly for quarters – that is when we would muster – uh, get together to see who was there."

The lawyer did not seem to notice that Will was treating him as someone who didn't speak English. "And were you friends?"

Mote harrumphed, finding the question naïve as did Perkins. The lawyer seemed not to notice.

"One would not describe the relationship between an officer and one of his sailors as friendship. We were not antagonistic and I spoke with Mote more than with the other sailors."

"Why was that?"

Will tried not to look at Mote but was aware that the younger man was smiling, obviously suddenly interested. "He is interesting and smart and he wanted to learn about the ship." Perkins winced at his use of the present tense.

"When did you leave the ship?"

"Me or Mote?"

"Mr. Mote and yourself."

Will realized that he and Mote both were stuck in the past, referring to one another as they did twenty-four years earlier. "Well, I left the fall of 1980. Mr. Mote left earlier, in the summer of 1979."

"You seem very sure of your dates."

"Well, one does know when one leaves another country and a ship. As for Mr. Mote, you must know that his departure was somewhat infamous."

"Yes, but I will ask you not to refer to those events now or at any time in court. They could be prejudicial to our case." The lawyer, for all his jock aspect, was no dummy. "Did you stay in touch?"

"No, until last month I knew nothing of Timothy Mote after 1979."

"Okay. Now, I need to work with you on your attitude in court. The defense lawyer will try to establish that there was not enough of a relationship between you two to cause a reunion after twenty-four years. Do you understand?"

Will did not like being patronized by lawyers – there was one exception, of course. Flatly, he said, "Yes, not only the witness but the circumstances must be credible and unimpeachable."

The younger man raised his eyebrows and slammed his lips into a frowning acknowledgement. "Exactly as a lawyer would phrase it."

Mote chuckled and winked at Perkins. Perkins felt himself smile. The lawyer saw the exchange. "Something I need to know?"

Mote slid forward, "Mrs. Perkins is a lawyer – good one, too."

"Ah," said the young lawyer, moving powerful shoulders in a loosening, circular motion, "but please excuse me if all this seems obvious, but we must still prepare you for the stand."

"Of course, Mr. Hepburn. My wife's the lawyer, not me."

"Okay, were you surprised when Mr. Mote called out of the blue last month?"

"How should I answer – I mean should I think of myself as being under oath?"

"Yes, but every truth has shades and shadows. Say the truth in the color that helps us."

Perkins looked at the lawyer, reevaluating. *Finally*, he thought, *language I can understand.* "Yes, I was surprised but not amazed. Life on board ship can be very intense – close quarters, shared experiences, a feeling of responsibility for one another, so we, that is to say those of us who have served together, often feel a desire or even a need to see one another, even years later."

"And such a need was what Mr. Mote felt, you believe."

"No, in his case, I think it was more interest and fun. Timothy Mote, if you'll excuse the pun, sailed through his Navy experience – probably even after he left the *Utica*. I think he wanted to enjoy a laugh about old times and see what I was doing. How'd you find me?" he asked suddenly, looking deadpan at Mote.

"Well, hell, lieutenant, you and I are both members of the Cruiser Association. I was just glancing at their membership and I saw your name. Easy then to find you in Boston."

"Were Mr. Mote's desires surprising or shocking?"

"Not at all, perfectly in character." *Does this lawyer suspect how much in character*, thought Will, who had a clear picture of scribbled notes with the whereabouts of any number of pigeons.

"Good, you see we must convince the judge that Mote's reasons for seeing you were understandable, normal, and even, to some extent, expected. Have other men from your Navy days shown up unexpectedly."

"No, but there have been some instances of unexpected contact in the form of a phone call or letter after many years. Six months ago a fellow officer sent me a letter with pictures of his family. I had not heard from him since the early eighties."

"No shit," the unrestrained Mote butted in, "who was that?"

"Mike Byers."

"Lieutenant Byers, with the little MG and the girlfriend from the gut? What was her name? Ah, I remember, Rose, but we called her Dandelion."

"Let us return to the discussion at hand," said the lawyer, laughing and amused at the exchange between the two.

"When Mr. Mote called, did he want anything specific?"

"He wanted to talk to me and suggested a bar and a time."

"Did you accept the invitation?"

"Yes and no. I had plans for the appointed time but met him at another time."

"How was the meeting? Did you find the situation awkward?"

Now it was time for Will to laugh. "Awkward? Petty Officer, uh, Mr. Mote does not make people feel awkward. He talked to me like a long, lost friend."

"What did you talk about?"

"Mostly the ship and those on it. He knows quite a bit about what happened to some other sailors. He was interested in my career and very interested to know how Mrs. Perkins was doing."

With a raised eyebrow, Hepburn pursued the teacher, "Why would he be so interested in Mrs. Perkins? That the two of them should have any kind of, for lack of any other word, relationship, seems unusual to me."

"Well said, Mr. Defense lawyer. It is unusual, but Beth, my wife, had little use for the distinctions between officers and enlisted and occasionally spoke with Mr. Mote those years ago. The two of them enjoyed one another's company, but there was nothing salacious. They are both bright people."

"I see. Go on with your conversation."

Mote butted in. "Yeah, and you remember, we talked about the gunner. How you had the watch that night. Remember?"

Will realized that Mote was being clever as usual. He was lost for words as he realized that that Mote had at once given him a conversation that he could remember and a more sympathetic view of his old 'shipmate.'

"Do you remember, Mr. Perkins?"

"Mote and I talked about the group of men with whom he associated. One of them was a diffident young gunner's mate who to this day we refer to only as the gunner. I don't even remember his name."

"Believe it or not, his name was David Jones."

The sailor's language returned to the teacher, "Holy shit, no wonder he was slow to tell people his name. Davy Jones on his way down to Davy Jones locker."

"Yeah, fucking ironic, isn't it?"

The conversation paused, Mote and Perkins transported back to visions of the nervous gunner while the lawyer shifted through papers to see if there was anything else. Finally, the lawyer spoke, "Perfect. Remember that attitude you have right now. Old, what word did you use?"

"Shipmates," chimed the other two men almost as a chorus.

"Yes, exactly like that. Two shipmates reliving old times – old times obviously still very vital and important to them. The prosecutor will try to poke holes in your testimony so make sure you use the same words and sentences over and over. You might even write them down. But answer naturally, off the cuff, take your time, don't sound rehearsed."

"I know my role here, counsellor. And I know what a good witness does for a case."

"Good words, lieutenant."

The lawyer shook his head at Mote's use of rank. "Yes, keep that Navy address in court, too. It sounds very convincing and bound to draw in a judge. We will draw up a statement for your signature." There was something much keener and deeper in the relationship between these two, the lawyer thought, but the only analogous relationship he could think of in his own life was his time with his fraternity brothers. "I need some time with you, Mr. Mote. Thank you for your time, Mr. Perkins."

"You're welcome." He shook hands with the lawyer and turned toward Mote.

But Mote butted in, "Hey, can I talk to the lieutenant out in the hall for a moment?"

"Of course."

The two shipmates moved into the red carpeted hall, Will going first, and Mote shut the door. "I already wrote out the sentences, just to make this little favor of yours a bit easier. You know, only part of this is a lie. All the stuff that happened to the two of us is true."

Will took the paper from the aging thief gratefully. "There were and are layers of truth and of relationships. Won't do to peel away too much. I am curious though. Did you commit an armed robbery?" He was standing away from Mote, the sweat returning to his hands.

Mote grunted, jerked up one side of his mouth, happy once again that the teacher spoke to him as an equal, but he had one more thought for his uncomfortable lieutenant. "Maybe I should tell you what happened to the gunner; I mean what I did for the gunner." His face was ugly and his eyes looking hard into Will's.

On his way home, Will reflected on this entire scene. *Layers upon layers,* he thought, and Mote was somehow writ large right to the core of the truth. He's a puppet master who knows how to make the puppet feel happy about his dance. *How many times have I danced for others? But not with Beth, no not for or with Beth. What will she think of me dangling on strings lying in court?*

## CHAPTER 20

# THE BEST LAID PLANS

WHEN ROSARIO, THE DISBURSING OFFICER, and their marine escort drove through the gates of the pier on D-Day at 1500, Manny knew that everything was going well. The marine on the gate did not want to let them in and the disbursing officer had to explain why armed men were coming on board. There were no sailors coming from the ship, and as they parked the car and he looked toward the ship, he saw men in OBAs (oxygen breathing apparatus) on the starboard side, obviously a damage control party, smoke coming from aft somewhere, a crowded quarterdeck. But there were also marines patrolling. The big disbursing clerk set his face rigid and tried to assess everything as they came on board and went down one deck and then aft toward supply. He was hoping that he'd been smart enough no matter if the heist was on or not. Was it foolproof enough to give him breathing room and a wad of cash? He had never admitted that he was part of the conspiracy, but had always prefaced any statement with, "Well, if we were really going to do this. . ." He had only met with Mote and Jervis. There was no paper trail, only the word of Jervis and Mote against his if all was not well.

Rosario's only role was to leave the safe tumblers where all someone had to do was turn the lever in the middle of the lock and rotate the tumbler to the right. He never questioned how Mote would get into the locked supply spaces. He would not be leaving the ship but find his share left in a locker in the Formia train station.

Mote was wrong about the gunner's location. The skinny petty officer was not ashore and not in his berthing area. The gunner was at the MAA shack where he dropped a note saying the fires were no accident and to find SM3 Mote. He was sure no one had seen him, but he was wrong. One of the marines, whose usual job was to stand sternly outside the XO's cabin, had seen the greasy sailor skulking around too much and throwing the paper into the MAA space. The marine was trained to be suspicious and he collared the gunner and handed the paper to the MAA.

The MAA ran to the quarterdeck. Perkins only glanced at the paper, but noticed his own sweat running onto the paper. He came close to the POOW and said slowly and loudly, "Tell the duty engineer to report on the water level in the bilges. Over the 1MC, call everyone not on watch or in a damage control party to quarters."

"Quarters, quarters, all hands not on watch or in damage control to quarters."

"Lance Corporal, go to the signal bridge and bring any of the SMs on watch to me here." The young marine looked confused. "Right behind the bridge where the big eyes are."

"Uh, aye, aye, sir."

Mote had decided that a little liberty was called for but was seen by the MAA from the quarterdeck before he got there. "The CDO wants to see you." On their way, Mote was remembering his own rehearsal admonition in the remote case that something went FUBAR: "Don't say anything. Ask for a lawyer." Inside he was kicking himself for making the most elemental of mistakes, that of choosing the wrong people. He had wanted to find those who had nothing to lose like Anderson and Jervis, or too much to lose like Washington and the lieutenant with his sophisticated wife. But then there was the gunner, who had nothing to lose but thought he did. He had lost his nerve or blabbed something.

The MAA marched Mote to the quarterdeck where he could not hide his surprise at seeing Lieutenant Perkins. A report was relayed from engineering, "Four feet of water in the bilges and rising. Engineering department is searching the spaces. We need more people down here."

Will took the 1MC himself. "All engineering personnel report to their duty stations. Engineering personnel on fire control parties should report to their duty stations when relieved. I say again, all engineering personnel report to their duty stations." He then turned to the messenger of the watch. "Run, and I mean run, down the pier. Get any snipes hanging around back on board NOW!"

Mote watched with a detached, but appreciative amusement. His lieutenant was a pretty good officer when he wanted to be, he was thinking. "Reporting to quarters, sir. I believe I'm the only signalman on board. Surprised to see you here, sir. I thought you and Mrs. Perkins were in Rome."

"Tomorrow." Will hesitated for the first time that afternoon. "Maybe. You've been identified as someone who might have something to do with the fires on board this afternoon."

Mote had already practiced his response in his head. Be scared but not too scared — you're innocent. "I'm sorry, sir. I don't think I can help you." He looked down and then nervously around, sloping his shoulders and looking as small and vulnerable as possible. So, he was thinking, *here's the silver lining. The lieutenant is going to protect himself and maybe me with him.*

The on board NIS agent arrived, followed by the XO who told them the skipper was on his way. The chief master-at-arms had meanwhile made his way to the quarterdeck. Perkins led the XO to port side where he gave him a report on the fires – slow going getting them under control with the fire main pressure low, the water in the bilges – difficulty getting all the valves turned since they had been rammed open; and the note about Mote. The XO was stunned but certainly knew he was not letting go of Mote. "Lieutenant, have the marines prepare the brig." The XO made his way back to the quarterdeck to find Agent Kelsey, "Signalman Third Class Mote is all yours."

As they frog marched Mote to the brig, the agent walked with him and warned quietly, "I'll need to ask you a few questions. You are being held on suspicion of arson. This is very serious and I recommend you tell the truth. Anything you do say could later be used against you at mast or at court martial."

Mote said nothing but carried out the orders of the marine to perfection.

Mote's escorts of two marines told Rosario to move aside as they manhandled the cuffed sailor toward the brig. Mote had on his usual "what, me worry" grin and slyly winked at Rosario. That was the last time Rosario saw him. He counted the money in the safe with the disbursing officer, the two of them checked that the safe and the spaces were properly locked, and DK1 Manny Rosario went below to study for his chief's exam.

# CHAPTER 21

# GOOD THINGS COME
# TO HE WHO WAITS

THE LIFE OF AN NIS (later the NCIS) agent is not always a glamorous one, full of forensic science, high level corruption, murder, and clever gangs; instead, it is a constant flow of minor security breaches, security checks, liaising with other law enforcement agencies, and giving advice to commanders. John Kelsey had been a naval officer, but decided that the life of a seagoing sailor was too hard on his family. So, he chose to become an NIS agent, only to be assigned to the *Utica* and head straight to sea, although admittedly not too long each time and to interesting ports, since this flagship was already homeported in the Med.

The evening that Mote was sent to the brig, Captain Donahue called Kelsey to his stateroom. Donahue was even more than would be expected of a flagship skipper. Somewhat unusual, he was not an academy grad, but had gone to Georgia Tech where he was an engineering major and tight end. Six feet four and powerfully built, he was nonetheless seldom intimidating; rather, he was known to be frighteningly smart and knew the ship and many of the crew like they were all family. Married with four children, he was still very attractive. Beth called him Captain Hercules. He had served his first class midshipman cruise aboard the *Utica* and this, his third command, was a dream come true. There is an old saw in the Navy that when an officer must do something he has not done before, a submariner will look at the regulations (regs) and if there is nothing that specifically allows him to act he will not. The surface sailor will check the regs and if there is nothing that does not allow him to act, he will. The Airedale (flyer) will act for it is easier to ask forgiveness than permission. Donahue was no stereotypical surface captain; he analyzed every situation on its own merits, sometimes wedded to regulation, but not afraid to go out on a limb. He was fair, hardworking, kind, and a wonderful ship driver. The crew generally loved him, and though his punishments at captain's mast tended to be harsh, very few could hold a grudge against him. In short, he was the last man anyone could imagine a plot against.

While Mote was in the brig, the skipper called the NIS agent to his stateroom and let him pass the marine guard immediately. The captain asked Kelsey to sit in a chair not two feet away. Kelsey, who himself was six feet tall, but thin with his dark hair thinning on top, felt small but also important. The captain told the orderly to fetch coffee, looked directly at Kelsey (unnerving at such close quarters) and asked, "What constitutes mutiny?"

Kelsey guessed correctly that with the flag JAG (lawyer) ashore, he was fulfilling the legal as well as police roll. With a calm, flat voice, in his best legalese, the agent replied, "Article 94 of the UCMJ lists three kinds of mutiny or sedition. The first is trying to overthrow authority by refusing to obey orders; the second is violence against a person in authority; and the third is failing to prevent mutiny when he or she knows it's taking place."

"So, is planning to destroy a ship mutiny?" The captain was drumming his fingers on his desk, obviously trying to sort out his plan of action.

"Well, sir, it's certainly a court martial offense and there is violence involved, so the officers of the court would have to decide."

Kelsey hoped he wasn't being vague or evasive. He was ready to get out of the hot seat.

Donahue considered Kelsey's answer and stopped drumming his fingers. "Well, John, let's say it's mutiny, because that's what it feels like to me. So, is knowing about a mutiny and doing nothing in itself mutiny?"

"With respect, sir, no it's not. It's stupidity." The captain laughed.

The marine orderly opened the door to let the XO enter. Always deferential and used to waiting to be asked to speak by his superior, this time the XO got right to the information in an obviously practiced speech. He was a perfect counterpoint to the old man; not large, but short; not white, but black; not kind-hearted but mean or so he and the captain liked the crew to believe. "Fires in both paint lockers and the helo deck are out, but the low fire main and skeleton crew made it all a challenge, especially in the helo deck. Lot of shit back there, black and ugly now. Power restored as you see and we're not sure if that was related. The bilges are being pumped out, but someone really knew what they were doing down there. Your old friend, CWO4 Romstedt, is still wandering around like the boiler room ghost looking for clues and saying he couldn't have done a worse job himself. No clues about who lit the fires, but the DCA is back on board investigating. All we've got is SM3 Mote and the gunner's mate."

"And the admiral?"

"The flag watch officer says he congratulates you on handling the situation well. The admiral will be in first thing in the morning to see you before he has a secure call with CINCUSNAVEUR."

"Any local press interest?"

"Nothing I know of, sir."

"Well, we'll let flag PAO handle that one. Thanks, XO. I want you to personally supervise the search of the ship and investigation into the fires and engineering spaces."

"With pleasure, sir." The XO turned to leave but quickly turned 180, obviously with one more thought. "Oh, skipper, Will Perkins did a helluva job containing all this. The boy's got a sixth sense for where disaster might strike."

"Roger that, XO. Sometimes those quiet ones can really step up to the plate. Now, John, where were we?" he asked nodding the XO away.

"We were talking about whether planning is mutiny. Unless there's some move to actually carry out the crime, it is not mutiny. Mutiny, after all, is so serious it can carry the death penalty."

Donahue leaned forward and bored into the agent with his grey eyes; Kelsey understood why the captain had been known as fearless in his football days. This, thought the agent, is what this captain looks like when angry . . . Donahue was speaking in a husky whisper. "A plan I've read calls for killing marines, lighting fires, scuttling the ship, and stealing the payroll money. Is that mutiny or not?"

Kelsey wanted to say 'yes.' His mind wandered through his recitation of the UCMJ. Had he missed anything? He could feel his face turning red and his eyes blinking before the glare of the captain. "Jesus Christ, sir, may I have a drink of water?"

"Of course," the skipper answered in a warmer voice, suddenly understanding that he had intimidated the agent, something he did not intend.

Kelsey managed to swallow the water given him by the captain. Speaking slowly with enough deliberation to ensure a perfect answer, he said, "Captain, some part of that plan must actually have taken place or have been underway. The example the UCMJ gives is that planning to start a bonfire and buying matches is planning; commission begins when someone lights a match and tries to light the bonfire. If I may ask, sir," ventured Kelsey, his mouth so dry he could hardly speak past the cottonmouth, "were the actions the XO talked about called for in this plan?"

"Yes, the fires, the sea valves open, ammunition to counter any security, and the loss of ship's power. I suspect the JAG will say the same as you. We just need to link the plan to its author and find all the bastards responsible. I am not a vengeful man, John, but some crimes and criminals have to pay as much as possible. That is the only right way to proceed. Find the truth and give us enough to lock these guys away where they can't hurt anyone." After a pause, a glare, and a deep laugh, "Or I might be tempted to take things into my own hands." The last punctuated by the captain showing his huge hands.

Kelsey appreciated the gallows humor and felt more at ease. "Yes, sir. Does the MAA have more information for me? I need to know how you, we, came by this information."

Captain Donahue looked sympathetic for a minute as he surveyed the sweating agent. "Read this first," he said handing over a blue binder filled with yellow, legal pad sheets.

Kelsey held in this hands 'Operation Plan Million,' codenamed 'Amsterdam.' Page one he saw was stamped Top Secret with the usual declassification information. "Good God!"

"Ha!" laughed Donahue. "I think more from the other side from God. One of them chickened out, and pointed us in the right direction. I think the author of this, SM3 Mote we think, was extremely proud of his work. We found it in his sea bag packed for a long trip. The thing is, that's a helluva good plan – these are guys I'd want on my side, but they're not. Call the MA when you want to talk to the snitch. What else do you need?"

Kelsey took what felt like too long to consider and saw the captain ready to speak. "Just time and permission to consult my superiors in the NIS."

"Use anything and anybody on or off the ship. Anybody even looks like they're not cooperating, ask them if they'd like to discuss the matter with me. Just figure out how we get them all and I get to cut off their balls."

"Yes, sir. I have no doubt I'll have full cooperation. Shall I get started?"

"Why are you still here?"

As he rose from his chair, careful not to touch the captain, he answered, "Thank you, sir," and feeling like Christmas, Halloween, and the seven horses of the apocalypse all landed at once.

Kelsey had no office on the ship, but carried his treasure to the 01 Officer's Country where he had a stateroom to himself that also served as his office. His thin, brown hair was flying in all directions as he pulled open the shelf that served as his desk, turned on the fluorescent light, and began to read and make notes. The OPLAN was phenomenal, written in the same syntax as any military OpOrder with a glossary of terms, annexes, and appendices. Some parts of it were pure whimsy, like the list of references which began with 'Bonnie and Clyde Manual of Authority Beating' and ended with 'The Sundance Retrospective: How I should have gotten away Scot free.' The purpose of the operation on page one was clear and succinct: "To take whatever action is required to acquire the payroll of the USS *Utica* and escape to Amsterdam without being pursued or discovered for four days after the theft."

*Four days*, thought Kelsey, *time enough to travel and disappear into a literal cloud of smoke in Amsterdam*. But who was involved besides the gunner's mate and signalman? Was this mutiny?

At this point Kelsey put aside his own feeling of being in a B movie, and his own disgust at anyone who would even contemplate killing a shipmate. He stood, stared in the mirror over the sink next to his desk cum chest of drawers, to see a man, disheveled and grim looking, even skinnier than his 150 pounds, shorter than his six feet, and certainly older than his 35. Time to pull himself together.

By 2030, Kelsey had finished the OpOrder, made his charts of planned events, and come up with his list of questions. Even with his knowledge of ships, he wasn't quite sure if the plan would work because so many rates were involved and many of the details were left to the conspirators themselves. Did they actually have the ability to get weapons, get the money, get the sea valves open, get the marines, get the fires going, get off the ship, and get away? Who knew of the plan? Step one was to find out how much the gunner knew about the plan and those involved. He called down to the MAA shack. The chief himself answered and reported, "On our way."

The gunner had been held in the brig next to Mote and came to Kelsey's stateroom visibly shaken and exhausted, but also relieved to be away from Mote, who kept muttering from the next cell whenever there were no marines within earshot that there should be honor among thieves and rats must be exterminated.

When the gunner arrived at Kelsey's stateroom, his fingers were bleeding where he'd chewed his nails away and he was breathing deeply and irregularly. Clearly, he was already close to a breakdown. Kelsey saw that he needed to get him calmed down and then find a way to allow him to talk without fear.

"Hiya, gunner, would you like some coffee or something to drink? Something to eat?"

The gunner stood even though a chair was offered, "No, sir, I'm okay."

"Please sit down," the agent said, pointing again to the other chair in the four-foot-wide stateroom. "Mind if I have some coffee? I've just been reading for the past couple of hours and my brain needs a little stimulation."

The gunner barely listened but managed, "Of course not, sir."

Kelsey opened the stateroom door and asked the marine assigned to him for the evening to go to the wardroom galley and get him some black coffee. "This is quite a piece of work you led the master-at-arms to."

The gunner was confused, having barely taken in his surroundings. "Sir?"

Holding up the note, "Do you deny leaving this with the master-at-arms?"

"I guess not, sir. Somebody must've seen me. Is that what happened?"

"Yes, it is." Kelsey was ready to get down to work. "So, as I was saying, this is quite a good read, very organized and well written. Did you know about this binder?"

The gunner finally spotted the binder on the agent's desk. His hands shook between his knees and his too-long chocolate hair hung over his eyes as he stared at the deck. "I guess I saw it lying around."

"In someone else's berthing area?" Kelsey saw the panic in the gunner and knew he had to go slowly and not push too hard.

"You seem a bit shaken up, gunner. Are you afraid of something or someone? Best to be as honest as you can be." Kelsey tried a smile.

The gunner had Mote's words about saying nothing and about honor among thieves running through his head. "Sir, do I have to answer? Can I have a lawyer or something?"

"Gunner, we're talking about possible mutiny aboard a United States warship. I'm scared too. I'm scared people are going to die and you're not going to keep them alive."

"The only person," and here the gunner looked up, his eyes red and his voice shaking, "who might die is me." He looked back down and began working at his left thumbnail with his teeth.

The NIS agent shook off a natural sympathy for the gunner and leaned in for his own kind of kill. "You need to tell us when all of this happened so we can protect you."

The gunner was so afraid that he was only vaguely aware of what the agent was saying. "What's going to happen to me? Am I going to prison?"

Kelsey saw that the gunner would tell him anything in exchange for safety. "Well, let's see," he said in his most relaxed and friendly voice, "what laws or regulations have you broken?"

Looking up, listening, "Sir?"

"These pages here call for a "sailor three", one presumes a gunner's mate, to illegally withdraw weapons from the armory and provide them to individuals who were going to set off an explosion in the starboard gun barbette and, if necessary, blow up the marine barracks, kill the OOD, and force their way past anyone who prevented them from leaving the ship with the payroll. Were you planning to carry out any of these actions?"

"No, sir, honest I thought it was like some sort of game, but then they got real serious and told me when it was happening and when I should have the guns and stuff for them. We even had a rehearsal but I never did it and I didn't know exactly what they were going to do." The gunner was speaking quickly, neurotically, gazing around the space, with a squeal for understanding in his voice.

"So, you admit this was all actually supposed to happen?"

"Am I going to jail, sir?"

"Gunner, I just get the facts straight, but I think you didn't actually do any of this and you may have prevented anyone else from doing much of it. The next step is to help us find the others. You see we could charge you with mutiny which is as serious as it gets, but only if you actually did some of this. Of course, it's also mutiny if you knew that someone else was going to commit this crime and you didn't do anything to stop them, but then, thanks to you, they were stopped." Kelsey leaned back and let the gunner stare at the picture of Kelsey's wife on the shelf and continue to look around the stateroom. Was he looking for a way out? "Who wrote this? Who wrote this OpPlan?"

The gunner was now sitting up and he had control over his hands and voice: "So, maybe, I won't be charged with anything? Maybe I'll be okay? Can I have some coffee, please?"

Kelsey opened the stateroom door to the knock and the marine handed in two cups of coffee. *Some good fortune and yet another smart marine*, thought the agent. The marine closed the door and resumed his vigil.

"Sure, here you go and right on cue. So, you didn't steal anything. Who were you supposed to give the guns, ammunition, and grenades to?"

"I didn't steal it. I didn't steal nothin'. I just liked being with them. Besides," he hesitated and looked sheepish, perhaps ashamed, "I don't have any combinations to the armory, just to the outside hatch. I couldn't give them that stuff."

Kelsey's mind quickly ran through the ramifications of this. The gunner did not see backing out as an option and he was so scared of Mote that he hoped to get him off the ship. "Sounds like you're in less trouble all the time. "Who is them?"

The gunner was certain that he did not want anyone to be able to say that he'd turned them in. Too dangerous. "I don't know, sir. I was supposed to wait at the armory till someone came. They said the password earlier in the day. Then I was supposed to hand over stuff and get off the ship. Even in the rehearsal, I didn't see the guy."

"Hmm, I didn't see a password in the OpPlan. Somebody must have given you the password and then said the password or written it earlier today."

"I don't know, sir. I never saw it or read it. Mote changed the password every day. The latest one was 'marriage day.'" The gunner looked up with his mouth open, drawing in breath realizing he'd used Mote's name.

Kelsey was again stunned by the complexity of the plan. "Like a big party?"

"If you say so."

"Mote wrote the plan? How did you know it existed? When did you see it?"

"I seen him writing it on the signal bridge before. Yesterday I saw him with it in his rack."

"Okay, thanks. I think we can get you out of your predicament here. After all, you're one of the good guys, aren't you? I mean you didn't do any of this for real, did you?" he asked slapping the blue binder. "You've actually prevented much of it from happening."

"So maybe I'll get a medal or something? Maybe I'll really be okay?" The gunner was pleading more than asking and he looked completely exhausted.

"Well, medals are not part of my job, but advice about charges against people is. I will recommend to Captain Donahue that you not be charged with anything, but I still need something from you. You're doing a great job. I'm proud of you." Kelsey had decided that no one had ever expressed any pride in the weasel of a gunner. "Now, I know you don't want to tell me, but it's really best if you tell me who else knew and who else helped with the OpPlan."

"It is Mote, I swear it is, and the big boatswain's mate, Jervis. That's all I know and my part of the plan and how we were supposed to meet on the road to Tit Mountain tomorrow to divvy up the cash." The gunner stopped and was very still and quiet. The specter of Jervis and '*THUNDER*' and '*LIGHTNING*' was too large, too close, and especially too powerful.

"Stay here," said Kelsey, pushing past the gunner and opening the door. "Lance Corporal, keep the petty officer right here." He ran to the MAA shack where the chief was playing Acey-deucy, the sailors' version of backgammon, with the first class. "Our second guy is a boatswain's mate, Jervis. Find out if he's aboard. And I need to see Mote. I'll be with the XO."

In the dim light of the XO's large stateroom, Kelsey dared to look at the bleary-eyed commander who was now sitting in his underwear on the edge of his rack. "We've got Mote for sure. The gunner has confessed it."

"Who else?"

"Big boatswain's mate, Jervis. The MAA is looking for him now."

"Tell them to let me know. If he's not on board, we'll get the Carabinieri and the shore patrol on him. Where's the gunner's mate?"

"In my stateroom, but I'd like him to stay in the brig for his protection. Good treatment, of course."

"Good idea. I'll clear it with the captain. When do you start with Mote?"

"Staff Sergeant Majewicz is bringing him to my stateroom right now, I believe."

"Majewicz, huh. Better Mote than me."

# CHAPTER 22

---

# PRIDE COMETH BEFORE THE FALL

THE BIG STAFF SERGEANT HAD Mote in handcuffs and shoved him toward the NIS agent's stateroom at 2130. Mote moved as nonchalantly as possible but his mind was working fast. He had cleaned his hands from the engineering spaces, but his uniform and hair were not in their usual uber-military appearance. He felt dirty. As he reviewed the OpPlan, he could find no errors. No, the plan was good, but all plans depend on the people to carry them out. Somebody fucked up. No, they knew what to do. No, somebody got scared. Gotta be the gunner. He didn't have enough to hold over him and the bastard just wasn't hungry enough. Or smart enough.

"Please sit down, petty officer. Can we take the cuffs off, please?"

"Don't want to, sir. He's a strong asshole."

"Just take them off and wait outside with the lance corporal. I'll call for help and you look twice as strong as him."

"Yes, sir. Don't mind tellin' you I hope you yell," he said as he pulled the cuffs against Mote's wrists. "That way I would need to use all reasonable force to subdue the suspect. Problem is sometimes I don't know my own strength."

The agent smiled and closed the door. Mote stood unimpressed and with a hint of a smile as he took the chair the agent offered him.

"I suppose you know why you're here."

"No, sir, may I ask who you are?" Kelsey was caught off guard. He was used to always having an easy upper hand and realized he had already underestimated Mote.

Kelsey sat back in his own chair and told himself to take his time. Boredom might be a good weapon. "Special Agent Kelsey, Naval Investigative Service. And you are Signalman third class Timothy Mote, charged with conspiracy, mutiny, attempted robbery, and attempted murder. Anything you say may be used against you in court proceedings. Do you understand?"

"Sure, I guess," said Mote. Did he try to play the 'special agent' or did he just stay quiet? He didn't look too sharp but then maybe that was the way he wanted to look.

"Do you understand what mutiny means?"

"Yeah, it means you think I'm a dumb shit," twinkled Mote, so far deciding to just have fun but give nothing away.

"No, actually, you just proved you're a dumb shit," smiled the agent, who also was disheveled by the night's events, but who had shaved and was clearly fresh and awake, "by playing silly games. This is no game. You are under arrest for crimes with serious consequences."

*Damn*, Mote was thinking, *maybe not much fun here. Play it straight, smart, and quiet.* He glanced around the room to see if anything there could give him information about how to play the man or the situation. Books on the desk perfectly lined up. No pictures, no posters, everything inspection ready. *Guy's a pro*, thought Mote. "Mutiny is planning to take over a ship."

"Good, and conspiracy?"

"Conspiring or planning with others in secret to commit some act or deed, usually an evil or illegal one." *That should impress the bastard.*

Kelsey said nothing and tried to show nothing in his face, but he was impressed with the signalman's unstuttering eloquence.

"Interesting idea to use the ship against itself. Ship's weapons to arm the conspirators and to eliminate the most efficient security force."

*Damn gunner*, thought Mote, *little chicken shit*.

"Ship's own pumps and sea valves to flood, damage, and possibly disable the ship."

Gunner didn't know that shit. Anderson wouldn't speak. Mote had to put on his most surprised face – an easy task considering his level of amazement.

"Ship's own supplies of flammable to get fires going. Ship's own supply of money to enrich yourselves. Ship's own antiquated electrical busses to make a loss of power believable. And ship's natural reaction and initial chaos to get away."

Mote sat passively and shrugged slightly.

"Oh, I'm sure you're wondering how I know so much. Of course, this is a copy and the real one is now in safekeeping," he said glancing at Mote for any reaction at the production of the OpPlan. This time he was not disappointed. For just a second, a look of panic, hatred, or perhaps both flashed across the signalman's face before he settled himself back to wide-eyed surprise. "This is quite a piece of work, but fatally flawed."

Mote was keeping to himself to stay out of a trap.

"The problem is there's no back up – no way to pull out if something went wrong. I do like the perfect OpPlan organization with the annexes and appendices. Even the language sounds like OpOrder 2000, although some of it is kind of funny like the references to movies. Still, it shows a lot of work and research. I learned some things about engineering, nothing real specific, but then that's the beauty of the plan, isn't it? You can sit there saying you don't know what all the valves in the engineering spaces do and be perfectly truthful. I wonder if just one person wrote all this. Maybe, but he had to have help. Of course, it's hardly perfect. I don't see any good communication to warn of discovery."

"Read the whole plan. Annex Kilo calls for an abort password." *Shit, the bastard's got me. Now I gotta find another exit plan.* Not missing a beat, he added, "It was all just fantasy. Something I did for fun."

"And who did you have fun with. Who are they?"

*Okay*, thought Mote, *they caught me at the armory. That means the gunner chickened out but the rest of the play happened.*

"Just me and the gunner. Just something to pass the time and a way to fuck with that gullible asshole. 'Course I never meant to do any of it."

"No, just like the fires in the paint lockers weren't supposed to happen. Who set them?"

*Back on top*, thought Mote. *They got me, but nobody else, unless you count that weasel.* "Oh, so that's what those damage control parties were all about?"

"Of course they were, petty officer, but you underestimated the damage control parties and the efficiency of the quarterdeck watch. How much did Jervis tell you about how he was going to set the fires?"

Mote said nothing.

One look told the agent that he was now staring at a brick wall. "Okay, enough for now. Staff sergeant," yelled Kelsey, "take the signalman to the brig."

"Yes, sir."

"Wait a minute. Just out of curiosity, what was the password to abort?"

Again, Mote's need to brag overcame his better sense. "The fid has landed."

"Very naval, petty officer."

In spite of the excessive 'reasonable force' that the MAA used to put on the cuffs, Mote managed a respectful smile at the NIS agent. Kelsey smiled back. There was something engaging and wonderfully dangerous about this young man.

## CHAPTER 23

# LEAD US NOT INTO TEMPTATION

MOTE WAS SOON OFF THE ship and in the brig in Naples along with Jervis, whom the shore patrol found in the gut clutching his sea bag and so drunk that all he could or would say was, "Gonna wait till he shows up." He had come without a struggle, obviously even more confused than intoxicated.

Will also was in a kind of shock; after the bilges were down to normal and the fires were out, and he'd made his reports to the XO and CO, he was emotionally drained. *What's the next fire,* he thought. Would the investigating officers see him as the great and good CDO who acted quickly and wisely, or as the great cover-up artist who'd helped design the plan for all this destruction? Beth, naturally, saw his worry and initially thought that he was just recovering from the shock that such a heinous crime could have been perpetrated on his watch. "Sounds to me like you did everything you were supposed to do. Haven't the CO and XO praised you and even talked about a medal?"

"Yeah, well, I don't want a medal. I don't feel heroic. I feel dirty." They were sitting late at night on their steps overlooking the sea. They had been there for half an hour, quiet as church mice while they listened to their octogenarian landlord serenade his second wife on the balcony just above them in a deep baritone. A hard heart would be needed not to feel romantic with a warm sea breeze, a clear Mediterranean sky and a bottle of Prosecco.

*Way to ruin the mood*, thought Beth, but she was trying to help her new husband out of something she didn't understand. "I don't understand. You did your duty. You did what you're trained to do."

*How much to tell her?* He could absolutely trust her, but did he want to show her just how weak and stupid he'd been. "Beth, Mote is in my division, so I feel responsible. And I spent a lot of time talking to him about how things on the ship worked. I doubt he could have planned everything without some of my ad . . ., uh, – telling him things."

"You're not that boy's father, Will. Educating him is not a crime, is it?"

Will looked out at the lights of the distant fishing vessels and felt his mouth twist into a lopsided grin. *Maybe she's right*, he thought. *Maybe I'm overthinking this, but then she doesn't know the whole story.* Only Mote knew the whole story and he wanted it to stay that way. "Nope, just twenty-twenty hindsight. Who would believe that the 'boy' as you call him, with all his fun and curiosity, could be so evil?" His voice cracked with emotion.

"Obviously not you, my husband. Can I tell you something I learned in law school?" She held his hand and nudged him until he looked at her. "The reason that juries take so long is often because some of the jurors take that time to come to an understanding that the nice people they've seen in the courtroom are capable of the most evil crimes imaginable. Not every criminal looks like a mad dog. The best are often the most charming." She squeezed his hand.

"Am I really one of the world's great innocents?" He leaned closer to her.

"Yes."

"And are you Mrs. Great Innocent?"

"Till death do us part."

Over the next couple of weeks, many sailors were taken off the ship to Naples for questioning before the special court martial that convened there. The ship remained in port and the admiral's visit to a fleet exercise was cancelled. Mote had done his job well. Aside from the gunner, nobody on the ship seemed to know anything. Will was one of the first called, much to his relief, because he had been the CDO and also because he was Mote's division officer. The court did little more than review the detailed ship's log on the day. When asked why he'd set guards on several spaces on the ship, Will had replied truthfully that he was afraid that someone was trying to attack the ship and he'd thought of the locations of the ship's soft underbelly. The captain in charge of the investigation did not seem too interested in the lieutenant's testimony, perhaps because he was in a hurry to get to those who might have been involved. He glanced down at the pile of papers before him and asked, "Did you ever have occasion to talk to Petty Officer Mote about anything other than his normal duties and responsibilities?"

*Here we go*, thought Perkins, just able to control his voice and nerves. "Yes, sir. He liked to talk and on calm days at sea we would talk about all manner of things."

"Specifically?" he asked quietly, almost bored, without looking up.

"He'd tell me about his misadventures ashore and when he was in high school, but he'd also ask about things I knew, like college, books I'd read, marriage. He also wanted to know more about the ship."

At this the captain looked up. "Did he say why he wanted to know more about the ship? Did you find his questions, shall we say, questionable?"

Will was glad of an easy question. "SM3 Mote is curious about everything and I believe he truly is interested in the organization and routines of the ship."

"So, let's get on," said the captain. "Did he ever say that he was going to start fires, or steal money or arms, or conspire to damage the ship?"

Will Perkins had listened carefully to the question. He paused and realized that the captain had said nothing about planning, only actual commission. "No, sir."

All the main conspirators testified before the court martial board, except the gunner, who was in such a state that he agreed to let the NIS agent Kelsey speak for him. This arrangement was acceptable to the court since the gunner was receiving medical attention for his fragile mental state. The gunner nodded 'yes' as Kelsey explained his role and he was released back to the ship, where the captain put him on restriction for his own safety and the appearance of punishment.

As for Anderson, CWO4 Ronstedt had looked for him the afternoon of the 'attack' since Anderson had the watch; the warrant had sworn blind that he'd kill him when he showed up. No one knew where Anderson was, only that he'd left the ship sometime before or right around the time of the fires. He came back the following morning in time for the muster of restricted men the next day, Saturday. His luck had run out because the MPA was the CDO and immediately turned him over to the MAA. During the questioning of the sailors, several said they saw him with Mote and Jervis, but the stories of the three conspirators on the fantail matched: not much conversation, just bumming cigarettes. When they did talk it was about their times ashore and occasionally about how fucked up the whole Navy was. But, he had left the ship while restricted; that was certain. The skipper threw the book at him: fines, more restriction, more extra duty, and a reduction in rate to BT3. When sailors are 'awarded' their punishment at mast, they salute and thank the captain. In Anderson's case, the gratitude was real for he didn't really care about money, restriction, or even his rate, as long as he could continue to have the ship as his home and go down to the boilers. There was something from Nelson's Navy about him – a sailor wedded to a ship.

EM3 Washington stayed with the party line that the shore power and telephones were unreliable, and he'd seen plenty of losses of shore power. His chief came to his rescue saying the EM3 was an excellent sailor who had already paid the price for one mistake.

There was no proof that Jervis had lighted the fires. He had been seen leaving the ship, but the times that sailors gave ranged from before liberty call at 1100 to around 1500. The preponderance of evidence indicated that he wasn't on the ship during the fires. Jervis could honestly say that he didn't know what was kept in the helo hangar (aside from the gasoline he put there) and fires in paint lockers are not unusual, even without an incendiary device. The gunner could not testify that he'd ever heard anyone talk about the OpOrder besides Mote; Jervis, the big deck ape, he said, didn't really contribute to the plan and didn't seem that interested. Jervis was let go without charge, but he asked for and was granted a transfer to another ship for his own protection. Everyone in the deck department was glad to see him go a month later.

Mote, himself, had never received the weapons and the only proof of any kind that he'd been or intended to be involved in some nefarious scheme was his OpOrder, for which he freely took credit saying it was just a fantasy that passed the time.

Nonetheless, the gunner's testimony, the completeness of the OpOrder, the remarkable similarity between the plan and the events of May 25, 1979, led the judge and three other officers of the court martial to find Mote guilty of a lesser offense, that of conspiracy, Article 81. Mote was reduced in rank to E-1, seaman recruit, confined to the brig for 90 days and dishonorably discharged.

Before his confinement in Naples, he returned one last time to the *Utica* to gather any last belongings. With his shore patrol escort accompanying him the entire time, he had no chance to say much to anyone, but as chance would have it, Perkins was the CDO again and LTJG Schmidt had the watch when Mote was due to leave with his few belongings. Prior to the obligatory turn to the colors and request for permission to leave the ship, Mote looked at his division officer and smiled, "Well, lieutenant I'll miss our chats on the signal bridge. They were, how would you put it, most instructive." Mote was twinkling with mischief as he saw his lieutenant's jaw set. "Of course, no one will ever know how much I learned unless I tell them. Someday, we'll have to relive old times and maybe you'll choose to repay me a favor. Oh, for now, please take care of this." Will found a brown envelope in his hand. At this point, Mote did not dare look threatening in front of the shore patrol who were paying scant attention, but his face and eyes did communicate a seriousness that the officer could not ignore.

So, what happens next, petty officer?"

"Cats land on their feet, lieutenant. There's a whole big world out there for a tomcat like me. I have permission to leave the ship," he said with his sharpest salute, smiling that he had used an officer's report to the OOD and had not asked permission.

Schmidt was taken aback at the petty officer's audacity, even though he really did have permission to leave the ship. Will took over and returned the salute, "Very well . . . and good luck."

As he headed down the brow, "And to you, sir. Fair winds and following seas." Mote's smile was genuine, but whether out of friendship to his division officer or pleasure at his own use of the standard Navy words upon departure was never clear to Will.

Later on in the wardroom drinking black coffee, Will lifted the flap on the brown envelope. Inside were 19 one-hundred-dollar bills and a note: "For EM3 Washington. Forgive me my (gambling) debts and fuck those who trespass against me." Will duly delivered the envelope, sure that Mote's confusion of the two versions of the Lord's Prayer was meant for him; Mote knew he'd have to open the package to see who should receive it and he knew that Will would read and understand.

# CHAPTER 24

## BETWEEN A ROCK AND A HARD PLACE

TO THOSE WHO LOOK ON from outside or those who have not been married for over twenty years, marriage seems like a hard-forged routine made of compromise. The truth is at once less dramatic and more romantic. No one married for a long time can tell you exactly how and when every ritual, routine, or private joke came to be. In fact, happily married people don't even think in terms of ritual or routine – it is simply their marriage. Every morning, Will brought Beth breakfast in bed. "Aw, how sweet," said those few people who knew of his morning chore. They did not know that he simply liked to get up in the mornings more than she and that her breakfast of decaf coffee, toast, and occasionally poached eggs was simple to make, while he prepared a more calorific morning feast for himself. Indeed, it was less romance than an understanding of their own ways of doing things and how to live without bumping into one another.

This morning, however, Beth rose first and brought Will eggs benedict. He was surprised, not so much at the breakfast, but at his own sleep past 6 a.m. and Beth's look of concern. "Thank you," he said. "Did you discover that I'm actually adopted and today is my real birthday?"

"No, not quite, but you haven't been this restless since you left the Navy. It was heavy rolls in the bed last night." She was sitting on the edge of the bed, dressed for work in wool trousers and a matching short jacket over a cream silk blouse and pearls. He sat in the bed in Mickey Mouse pajamas, a gift from her.

"Yeah, it's Mote haunting me."

At once the attorney and the loving wife, she leaned toward him, "You need to tell your personal counsel who happens to be your wife the full story." Beth remembered Will's relief when Mote had left the ship all those years before. She couldn't remember any conversations about him since Will himself had left the Navy. She deduced from the way he spoke about Mote that he still simultaneusly liked and feared the younger man. It really did feel the same as when Will was called to Naples to testify about Mote.

*Where to begin*, he thought, before looking wearily and sadly at the woman he loved. "Tonight, dinner at the Four Seasons, a bottle of wine, and I'll spill my guts." He tried to smile.

She was more successful than he at knowing that once he had decided to come good, then maybe she could get some sleep and he could find some peace. "Okay, my captain, but don't go UA on me or I'll send the SPs for you, just like the old days." She winked, kissed him routinely, and went to work.

The old days, he was thinking, were truly halcyon days for Beth, but did she have any idea of his sinking feeling that issues from those days were unresolved, not only his relationship with Mote but his entire vision of himself?

That day in the third period class of AP Language, Clarence, the smart but mischievous one, with his long, sandy hair and Nirvana t-shirt, decided he was tired of hearing Mr. Perkins' examples of writing with passion, of creating and articulating a voice. They were supposed to write reviews of books about which they felt passionately one way or another. For Clarence, whose passions lay in electrons flying through cyberspace and in fantastic games peopled by muscled monsters and thinly clad babes, the assignment had been difficult. "Mr. Perkins?"

"Yes, Clarence?"

"I need to have more examples. Maybe you could tell us about your passion for a novel."

*Damn that Clarence*, thought Will, *he can sniff weakness.* Probably learned from some damn Dungeons and Dragons game. Normally, this experienced teacher would have told the boy to see him after school when Will would have time to answer fully, knowing full well that the boy would never give up his own time. But today Will was truly full of passion, and he felt a welling of feeling that was too hard to keep down. He sat on the edge of his desk, facing the class, a rare pose for him since it implied both informality and superiority. He sat still for what seemed a minute, jutted out his jaw and began quietly, "In Joseph Conrad's *Lord Jim*, the eponymous Jim makes a mistake as a young man and spends the rest of his life trying to prove himself worthy. And he is worthy to the point of earning the name, even the title, of Lord Jim. Still, in the end he cannot accept himself as worthy or courageous or even good, much less lordly, so he carries on in a foolhardy way in the face of adversity and destroys himself.

"How many of us are Lord Jims? How many of us are haunted walking down the street by a random shot of guilt or embarrassment from the past? Maybe it was something we said or didn't say. Maybe it was a crime of omission when we had a chance to do something good, even honorable, and did not. Or maybe it was a spark of laziness or childishness or even evil that caused us to hurt someone.

"Generally, we are constructed to lose the worst of our memories so that we can carry on, but for some of us, for Lord Jim, one memory subsumes the rest and consumes the present. He is not Lord Jim. He is the boy who was cowardly while dreaming of bravery. It is the first of his waking thoughts and the last of his dreams – that he failed, that he is not worthy, excuse me young women, but he feels he is not manly.

"When I read *Lord Jim*, I am overcome with a sense of humanity never living up to its visions of itself, or each of us hurt by our own consciences, by our own ugliness, by our own weaknesses, and that dark heart of a memory is what we will see when we die as it blots out a lifetime of trying to do the right thing." He paused for just a second, sat up and looked directly at Clarence. "How do we survive once we know that we are not and cannot be Lord Jim?"

Will glanced at the silent class for only a moment and then stood, walked around his desk, and straightened papers. "You have ten minutes to write." Clarence, meanwhile, looked down. He realized he had gotten more than he bargained for, that a ploy for a simple detour from routine had unleashed the waters of a dam. And the dam had washed over him, for there was nothing in his games that contained any of the passion of his teacher whose usual quiet, deep, controlled voice had been hard, challenging, and full of pain.

The Four Seasons Hotel is on the south side of Boston Common and looks out or perhaps imposes itself over this pretty part of Boston. The maître d' is not quite as haughty as those in Masterpiece Theater but certainly makes the Bostonians occasionally think of their former English masters as they are shown to their tables laid with fine linen and flowers. Beth often had afternoon tea there, but a full blown dinner was an extravagance for Will and a welcome treat for Beth. They ordered the house white and perused the menu. Choices over, Beth waited for her husband to begin but soon decided that a prod in the form of a kick under the table would break him out of a reverie and mood that was at best tangential to the present. Will grunted, "I suppose I deserved that."

Trying to be light and playful, Beth answered, "I don't know. Have you been carried away by one of those buxom young scholars of yours?"

Will half smiled and put his hands palms upward on either side of the rows of cutlery. Looking from one hand to the other, he finally looked up at his smiling wife with moist eyes to say, "No, that does sound pleasant, if unprofessional, but there was a smart young man, one of those math types, who tried to get me off topic today and succeeded. I gave him and the class five minutes of verbal diarrhea about Lord Jim and leading a life trying to atone for a mistake.

Will began to speak as if from a memorized text, which close to the truth. "The reason Mote was admin discharged from the Navy was that he wrote and almost carried out a masterful plan of mutiny, murder, and robbery. He talked to me about it. I suppose I was part technical advisor and part editor. In either case, he always said that the plan would never have come into being without me. When he was caught, he managed to protect his co-conspirators, none of whom knew that I had any role to play at all. When he left the ship, I had the quarterdeck and he whispered to me, 'You owe me, lieutenant. And you know what payback is.' That's what this is all about – payback."

By this time Beth had interlocked her fingers, leaned forward, and was breathing into the fists of her hands. She moved her fingers under her chin. "Okay, so what is the payback?"

With no hint of humor, Will looked above her head, "Payback is a motherfucker. Mote is using me as an alibi. He's been charged with some robbery and I'm to swear, perhaps in court, that he and I were having a drink one afternoon, February 8, 2002, I think, before you got home. Supposedly we were telling sea stories and reliving the life of shipmates."

"And where was he, in fact?"

"I don't know. Obviously, he's in need of an alibi and I have a sense that this is not the only time he's been in court since the summary court martial that sent him out of the Navy."

Beth was trying to piece together a story that she was coming to realize was a deep part of her husband. *Talk about women keeping secrets*, she mused to herself. "Charges? What were the exact charges against him all those years ago and what in the world has that got to do with us now?" She waited for Will's eyes to stop searching the room for an escape and for him to show enough empathy to realize that Beth had been in the dark for so long that she barely knew any of the story. "So, why in the world would you perjure yourself and possibly ruin you and me for him?" An edge was developing in Beth's voice, an impatience, as she struggled to keep Beth the lawyer at bay.

Will sighed, "I do owe him. Please understand. He and his friends were going to disable the ship, steal the payroll, and head to Amsterdam. It was a very well thought out plan. You probably know or at least suspect that all those years ago when he was sent off the ship that I had something to do with his failed plans. He ran everything by me. I'm sure I must have helped him in some way and he believed we were away that weekend when he was caught. He could have easily ruined our lives. If he'd implicated me, my life, our lives would have been completely different. I could never have become a teacher and who knows what earthquakes we would have suffered, or even if we would have survived. Instead, I got a Navy Commendation Medal for my quick actions foiling a plan that I'd helped to form."

Beth's legal mind and protective instincts both came to the fore. She wasn't buying any debt that Will felt he owed and it was her turn to take Will out of his usual 'make no enemies' self into a more courageous position. After all, he'd certainly done the same for her. "First of all, I don't have any proof that you were actually in any way responsible for his actions, only for his thoughts. Second, our lives are not going to be ruined by some maniacal petty thief. And third, has it not occurred to you that perjury could effect the same disaster as the one you think you avoided? And lastly, could it be that *he* owes *you*?"

Not quite a hammer blow to the temple, Beth's words nonetheless made him for the millionth time come face-to-face with the reality of his wife's legal mind. Her face showed little evidence of the sympathy she felt inside as she stared at him with wide eyes and shallow breaths. "Please go on," he said.

Beth hesitated trying to balance a need to speak to his state of mind and the danger to their marriage but also to focus on the consequences of his impending actions? "Well, perjury is often discovered and can carry a jail sentence. End of teaching career. Why? For misplaced, and may I say, ancient guilt. May I ask you to consider me in all this?" She leaned toward him and he had to force himself not to back away. "Not so great for the lawyer's reputation either."

Silence. Beth staring and Will sipping his wine looking down. *Surely,* he was thinking, *she knows that there's more involved here than just legal crap. And there's more to fear, also.* Beth broke the silence. "Were there others who he also protected?"

"You know there were."

"Do you think he's exacted a similar retribution from them?"

"Well, not with Washington, the EM, but Rosario and Jervis and Anderson would hurt him rather than hurt themselves."

"Well . . .?" pleaded Beth, her impatience showing as she ran both her hands down the sides of her head, holding her hair against the back of her neck.

Will sighed, blew through his lips, and let go what he thought was his hammer blow. "Yes, but there's also the gunner."

Beth squinted, trying to retrieve twenty-year-old memories and the last time she heard her husband say 'the gunner' with the same pathos. She put her hands palms up on the table. "Look, you've gone over all this. What? One hundred times? Is this the boy who went overboard?"

"Sorry," and he meant it. He was beginning to feel some relief actually telling the tale that he had indeed gone over, not one hundred times, but at least a thousand times since that night. "Okay. I had the watch and the deck. There was a man overboard. It was the gunner who was involved in Mote's schemes to steal the ship's payroll. I don't know how far Mote's charisma extends, but I feel that this was no suicide."

They ate silently and well, both of them making several escapes to the wine. After dinner, they skipped dessert in favor of coffee and brandy in the lounge, where they sat next to one another.

"We should do this more often," ventured Will.

Beth looked at him open mouthed for a second and then laughed loudly. "Well, now that your sense of humor has returned, here come the questions."

"Are you armed?" He squinted back. "Okay, then shoot."

"Do you think Mote really intends any payback? Or is he using you because he can, just as he did twenty years ago?"

"Well, yes, of course he's using me to get what he wants, just like before."

"Do you think that any of Mote's goon friends will ever touch you?"

"Probably not – we're too far from their worlds."

"So, perhaps the real reason you're even considering perjury is something else?"

Will considered, not whether his wife knew his reason, but whether she really felt the depth of his sense of impending betrayal. "Yes, I feel guilty and I think I should feel guilty. Maybe I led him astray. Maybe some stupid need on my part to feel liked and importnat caused me to enable his crime. I like him, Beth. I feel a connection to him. And I think he likes me, too."

Instinctively, Beth waited. Crossed arms and legs held in the tirade that she was ready to unleash if her sweet man did not come to his senses.

He gave her a crooked smile. "But I love you, Beth, more than all the mutineers in history. Trust me, please."

## CHAPTER 25

# THE DARKEST HOUR IS JUST BEFORE DAWN

A MONTH AFTER THE DEPARTURE OF SM3 Mote and a week before Jervis was finally transferred, Will was preparing for his watch as the OOD. They were independent steaming from Gaeta to Toulon where the ship was due to go into the shipyard for a few weeks. He had been to CIC down below to look at the radar situation and talk to the watch officer; he had seen that there were no contacts within ten thousand yards and they were thirty minutes ahead of PIM (projected intended movement). There was only one course change, twenty degrees to port, during the upcoming watch and he was looking forward to a quiet time with his thoughts. It was 0330 and he had the four to eight watch so he would get to watch the sunrise. He climbed the ladder the ten decks from CIC to the bridge, looking up into a dark world. With an overcast sky, no light anywhere was discernible to Will as he stood at the back of the bridge, hearing the quiet voices of the crew while he waited for his night vision to come. On such calm seas and with so little to do on watch, Will could really enjoy the magic of his eyes as they slowly adjusted, first seeing the red lights of the bridge, then the shapes of the sailors, and finally the details of the helm, lee helm, captain's chair, radar, navigation table, and the calm, sleepy faces of the seven men on the bridge and the port and starboard lookouts. "Hey, Will, you ready?" the off-going OOD asked him. "Nothing going on, ahead of PIM, and my rack is calling my name – 'Mike, Mike, come to me, come to me, my lover.'"

Will laughed, scanned the captain's night orders, checked that the chart had been well kept, looked over the log, took one last look at the radar, scanned the horizon port and starboard with the WWII vintage (and standard issue even in 1979) binoculars, and wandered back onto the bridge to his jokey fellow officer: "I am ready to relieve you, sir."

"I am ready to be relieved."

"I relieve you, sir."

"I stand relieved. This is Lieutenant Byers, Lieutenant Perkins has the watch and the conn."

"Aye, aye sir."

"This is Lieutenant Perkins, I have the watch and the conn."

"Aye, aye, sir."

Byers disappeared down the ladder and Will took his post at the stand-alone compass on the center line of the ship, thinking of the weeks ahead when the ship was in France for repairs and he and Beth would be in their little rented flat in Toulon where she could practice her French and he could perhaps even read a bit. The month had been a nervous one for both of them, as every night he was home Will would beat himself up recalling the details of all his conversations with Mote and all the suggestions he had made for the plot against the ship. When he had duty, he slept even less, wandering the ship from bow to stern, from bilges to flying bridge, all with the excuse that the CDO needed to make a complete tour of the ship. Will's role in the conspiracy, if he'd really had a role, remained covered but he still felt guilty, accused, and shackled by guilt and fear. Beth spent three nights watching him pace and then walk slowly and alone to the beach below their apartment before demanding that he tell her what was torturing him, even though she already knew. Before he could answer, she said, "That's all past. I'm here now and we're going home soon. Did you make that sailor commit a crime? I am here and you need to trade those bad dreams for a good one with me."

"Yes, counsellor," he had said, amazed at her calmness.

On the bridge now he was thinking that her calmness was actually relief at knowing for certain that what was going on had nothing to do with her. *What a remarkable woman*, he thought. The lawyer Beth guessed that the truth was worse than he had said, but the loving wife had repressed a legal mind and soothed both the fear and ego of her husband. He smiled to himself.

A yell from the boatswain's mate: "Aft lookout reports, man overboard starboard side"

"Hard right rudder. All engines ahead full."

"Hard right rudder. All engines ahead full, aye, aye sir."

As the big ship listed to port with the turn, Will boomed, "Bos. Announce man overboard. This is not a drill."

"Man overboard, starboard side," came the booming, nerve-shattering call over the 1MC. "This is not a drill, this is not a drill. Man overboard starboard side."

Will had checked the ship's heading as 330 before he had gone to the starboard bridge wing to conn from there. He had gone into automatic, somewhere the procedures for a man overboard turn taking over his consciousness even though he had only practiced such a turn once before. He had come hard starboard in order to swing the ship's stern and propellers away from anyone in the water. Now he was waiting for the ship to come to heading 030, 60 degrees from the original heading. "Shift your rudder, steady on course one five zero," he ordered down the speaking tube from the bridge wing, just when the skipper appeared with just his pants and a t-shirt on. "Report from the aft lookout that a man was overboard to starboard. I'm coming around to a reciprocal course. No contacts within ten thousand yards, sir."

"Very well, this is the captain, I have the conn."

"Aye, aye, sir."

The ship slowed to five knots as they came around to a reciprocal course and the motor whale boats were ready to launch. The ops boss sent an immediate message to the fleet HQ and briefed the flag watch officer on board. After a half hour's search, they had swung round to put the wind off the starboard bow and launched the SH3 helicopter. At the same time, the skipper told the bosun to announce quarters.

"Quarters, quarters, all hands to quarters." Just fifteen minutes later, the report came from the weapons officer that a gunner's mate was missing. Will knew before the information was relayed to the bridge to be logged. It was the first time he could remember hearing the gunner's name. He also knew that Jervis had not been on watch that night and that he himself was on the verge of tears.

The search continued throughout the next day and had been joined by Italian search and rescue helicopters. The only sign of the gunner were his boots just outside the bosun locker where Jervis 'lived' and a well-made rack with a wooden cross laid on top of a photograph of the gunner in elementary school standing next to his mother. He was never found.

Will, meanwhile, had been relieved of the watch. He went to the main deck to stare into the morning sun that was just visible through an unusually cloudy day. He crawled into his own rack without any breakfast, put the pillow over his head, and started to cry just before exhaustion took over and he passed into a nightmare world of sailors grinning and pointing at him.

## CHAPTER 26

# DUTY, HONOR, COUNTRY; OR EVERY DOG HAS ITS DAY

THERE ARE TIMES IN BOSTON near the old courthouse and Faneuil Hall that the cobblestones echo with the ghosts of those excited colonists who were full of an understanding of the possibility of a joyful new world, a good place to die if necessary. Will normally heard the ghosts late at night when the revolution was seething in secrecy and lurking in the corners of the solid bricks of the eighteenth century, but today he heard crowds massing, emotions welling up, freedom being shouted. The sun shone high and warm, the purple crocuses were out, the tourists were wearing Red Sox t-shirts and it was springtime.

Will was unusually moved by the history of those proud and reckless colonists over two hundred years before. Without his thinking, his feet took him to the courthouse where Mote's lawyer met him and escorted him to a seat outside the courtroom. Since the crux of Mote's defense depended upon Will's testimony, the wait was not long. The policeman escorted him to the witness stand where he was sworn in. He looked over to where Mote was sitting, well dressed in a blue suit, white shirt and black tie, almost like a Navy uniform. The younger man allowed the corners of his lips to hint at a smile.

The defense lawyer was saying good morning and explaining that he needed to ask a few questions to determine Mr. Mote's whereabouts on the evening of February 8, 2002. He was asking when and if he had seen Timothy Mote recently.

Will heard the question again, "When did you and Mr. Mote meet recently? Were you with him on that date at the Old Courthouse Bar?"

There was a shuffling in the room, but Will could hear nothing. He saw only the fleshy lips of the defense lawyer mouthing the question he had heard in his sleep and been waking to for weeks since the meeting at the opera house. He looked at Mote and saw him leaving the *Utica*, his sea bag thrown over his shoulder, and his Dixie cup hat tilted beautifully and defiantly onto the back of his head. "I have permission to leave the ship," Mote had said, head back, blond hair hanging down his forehead, a chuckle in his voice, using the words reserved for officers appropriately enough since he really did have permission to leave the ship and the Navy. "Remember, someday I'll need a favor and you owe me. Payback is a motherfucker."

**Mote was barely aware of the court proceedings as he slowly and meticulously planned a comeuppance for his current partner who had grassed on him, but when he turned to glance at Perkins, he met the eyes of his former division officer and suddenly sat straighter.** *I'll be damned,* **he was thinking,** *the son of a bitch has found his steel. He might just be going to give me the fid.*

*Payback is a motherfucker,* Will was thinking. *Is this when I am free of Mote and all those others who can make me feel my resolve turn to jelly merely with a strong look and stronger arm? Or am I doomed to be the pigeon, always surviving but fleeing at the first hint of personal challenge, if not physically, then in my chicken heart?*

**Mote thought back to a conversation all those years ago on the bridge wing one mid-watch. He remembered many of their conversations because he had never before or since talked to**

anyone on the subjects in the way Perkins and he found time while staring at the sea.

"So, lieutenant," he had said, "we're supposed to be out here defending the world from the red threat and all that shit, and we're supposed to be ready to lay down our fuckin' lives for President Ray Gun. You gonna do that? You gonna die for that prick?"

"No, not for him, but I have sworn to my commission and part of that oath is the understanding that I could die serving. It's not Reagan, it's an entire history and culture and progress toward decency and civility that we die for."

"Bullshit, you need to give up on that shit. Those motherfuckers are just like me – they do for themselves. The difference is that they got the power to make us die and they get away with it."

"Mr. Perkins, the court is waiting. Your shipmate, Timothy Mote, is waiting for you to release him from these scandalous charges."

*Scandalous charges,* thought Will. *What about the scandal in my gut? Maybe the motherfucker of payback will pay back all those times of quiet humiliation not being bold enough to follow my own heart and brain because of weak knees.*

"No, I did not meet Timothy Mote on February eighth." Will looked only at the judge, trying to speak loudly, but finding the sound of his voice amplified like the speakers in a small cinema. He could see himself speaking and hear the words, but like a numb onlooker, powerless to stop or think. The courtroom sounded like a classroom muttering before a test. *Nah,* Mote was thinking, *the old lieutenant is gonna drag out that Pollyanna crap about truth and honor and screw me to the wall. I shoulda known better than to trust an honest man. All those years I thought I had a wild card in my hand, saving it for just the right time to play it, but this one-eyed jack isn't wild. Maybe he never was. What did he say?*

"Well, I'm sure we all act in our own self-interest, but the best of us know that our lives and actions can be greater than ourselves, and for those people happiness and fulfilment cannot be met by selfishness."

"So, you're some kinda hero, waving the big flag for America, truth, justice, and Superman and all that bullshit?"

"No, but I wish I were. I'm a follower, Mote, you know that. I wish I were better than myself."

The idea of a man being better than himself clanged in Mote's mind as he watched the lawyer try to discredit Perkins. *Good show, this one,* he was thinking. Mote relaxed, moved into movie-watching position with his arms and ankles crossed, ready to find fault with the continuity.

Perkins did not look like a tower of strength, like a man who could stand up to the practiced and natural intimidation of someone like Mote. He was telling the truth but only his eyes looked strong. His shoulders were hunched and his fingers were shaking. He looked at the judge. "Here is a list of all the dates and times I met with or spoke to SM3, uh, Mr. Mote since he left the *USS Utica* in April of nineteen seventy-nine. All the dates are after the supposed meeting at the Old Courthouse Bar: phone call on February twenty-fifth; meeting at the Boston Opera House on March first; phone call on March twelfth; meeting in the office of Mr. Mote's lawyer on March twenty-seventh; and a phone call three days ago, April first."

"Your honor," interrupted the defense lawyer, "I have here for the court's review a signed and witnessed statement from Mr. Perkins which says that he and . . ."

"Your honor," blurted Will, surprised at his loud audacity, "I did sign that statement. I did sign that statement but it is a lie. Here . . ."

"Your honor, the truth is that Mr. Perkins is an unreliable witness. Move to strike his testimony from the record."

The judge seemed to almost be winking at Will as he shifted in his seat and leaned over to say, "Do you have any proof of your real whereabouts on February eighth?"

*All right, here comes the alibi,* thought Mote. *Has he put together his plan well enough for the truth to work? Or was he dumb enough to think he could just take it all back.*

*Yup, here it comes. 'I was home with my wife.'*

"I do, your honor. I was teaching a night-time SAT review session. Here is the sign-in sheet for students on that evening. Any one of them can confirm that from seven to ten that evening I was in my classroom."

*Damn, good one,* the accused was thinking. *No one's going to call in a bunch of kids and it's all too good. That's what I thought – all too good – until that bastard gunner turned us in. Maybe Perkins would have, too. Nah, but he would have puked out the truth if anyone had asked him just like he's doing now. He probably thinks he was part of us, that we trusted him, but he's wrong. I only trusted him to feel dirty talking to me and to keep his mouth shut. But I got lucky that no one else knew we talked. The son of a bitch charmed me and he never even knew he was doing it. He never really knew that he was the only intelligent guy on that ship worth talking to, that I used to think up crap to ask him, just to watch him squirm out those words, words that no one else I knew used or had even heard.*

"Your honor . . ."

"Mr. Perkins' testimony will remain on the record. The student log-in sheet will be accepted by the court. Do you have any further questions, counsellor?"

"Yes, your honor. Mr. Perkins, has the prosecution contacted you with regard to your testimony or documents?"

"No. Today is the first time I have seen the prosecutor."

"Have you discussed this case with any lawyer or counsellor?"

"No, uh, yes."

"Well, which is it, yes or no?"

"Your honor, I have discussed this case in general terms with my wife, who is a lawyer."

**Mote sat more upright and paid closer attention. He thought about Beth.** *Oh, shit, yes the wife. I remember what she was like then – pretty, walked with her head back, not afraid of sailors. What'd she see in him? Dumb ass – she saw what we're seeing right now – the guy who actually believes in honor. What did he tell me about honor – that honor is a task master, that it has caused people throughout history to act so that they would not shame themselves or their loved ones, that it has saved untold lives and taken untold lives but it is not personal; it moves in the sphere of radical importance beyond the grasp of the dirty fingers of little men. Dirty fingers of little men, like my lawyer there who's getting screwed to the wall by the old lieutenant. He's gonna win you dumb bastard. All that good shit inside him is gonna explode right in your face.*

"So, you have changed your testimony after consulting with counsel?"

"If you are treating my wife as my lawyer, your honor, then surely our conversation is protected by lawyer/client confidentiality."

"So, counsel advised you to perjure yourself?"

"No, as I recall," said Will, feeling the joy of the upper hand for once in his life, "she said she didn't know why I was going to be testifying since I hadn't told her anything, but to remember I was under oath and to be careful of the prosecutor, because he's a weasel."

**Mote laughed loudly at the description of the lawyer as a weasel, but also at his own predicament of being caught by his own underestimation of Perkins. He was appreciating the irony of being condemned by someone who was only there because Mote had involved him.** *What was that weird phrase he taught me – yeah, yeah, got it 'hoist with my own petard' – blown up by my own explosives trying to get into the castle.*

The judge's eyebrows jerked toward the ceiling before he broke the silence, "Any further questions, counsellor?"

"Not at this time, your honor," glaring at Will who glanced back.

"May I cross examine, your honor?"

"Please do."

The prosecutor, so recently described as a weasel, stepped up to Will with a quick, light step. "Mr. Perkins, there are some things the court needs to . . ."

"May I tell the nature of my meetings with SM3 Mote since nineteen seventy-nine? I think doing so will answer your questions."

"Continue," said the judge, almost kindly.

**Mote sat as if daydreaming; in fact, he was remembering another conversation from twenty years before. It was the one where he was sure he could really make the lieutenant squirm.** *Yeah, he thought, maybe I should have figured out that this pigeon wasn't gonna fly the time I tried to shock him by saying I didn't believe in God. Instead of shock, the lieutenant had laughed and said something like,* "Somehow I didn't think you did. Excuse me, petty officer, but I rather think you only believe in yourself." *That was a good one – a good shot, but not as good as what's happening right now. Yeah, then I tried to pin him down about his own religion, get him to admit that he was Catholic or some weird shit like that.* "But you're one of them believers, go to church and pray." *Nope, I had him all wrong. He wasn't no Sunday school type, more like a grown-up Boy Scout.*

"Mr. Mote called me on February twenty-fifth of this year. He said he'd done me a favor and now it was time for payback. On March first, before the *Cinderella* ballet, he gave me a piece of paper on which he had written down the time and details of a supposed meeting at the Old Courthouse Bar on February eighth. He said I was his alibi and I needed to commit the details on the paper to memory. The next time I heard from him was when he told me the arraignment had been set and I needed to see his lawyer. After we entered the office, Mote gave me the statement and told me I'd written it. He called one more time three days ago to remind me of an unfortunate event in nineteen seventy-nine when a young sailor went overboard."

Will again slipped into a previous life, feeling the ship turn hard to starboard and then hearing the nightmare call of the 1MC, "Man overboard. Man overboard starboard side. This is not a drill." He had executed the man overboard turn perfectly. By 0430, the sleepy signalmen were shivering in the breeze of the signal bridge during the obligatory quarters called to discover who was missing. No one had seen anyone go overboard, but the alert after lookout had seen something float by that looked like a man waving good-bye.

The prosecutor paced for a few seconds, "What was the significance of that event?"

"Sorry," said Will, dragged forward twenty years by the tone of the prosecutor and the vision of Mote leaning back in his chair, arms crossed, with that same look of amusement whenever someone surprised him. "The sailor who went overboard was a friend of Timothy Mote's and many believed that Mote had his other friends throw him overboard because the gunner had turned Mote into the NIS for plotting to rob and murder."

*That stupid gunner. That stupid deck ape. He didn't know enough to figure out that it was time to quit, to shut up and take a beating. Instead he chucks the gunner over the side. I should have killed him. Nah, not my style.*

"Move to strike that last statement and not germane to this case," the defense lawyer interrupted.

"I'll allow the statement to stand. We need to have the full story on record."

"And so you took his threat seriously because you believed Mote had killed this man?"

"No, SM3 Mote did not kill the gunner, but he may have arranged for someone else to do it, and yes, I was afraid."

Mote slipped back into his reverie. *I think I was the one who was kind of shocked by what he said, "No, Mote, I don't believe in God, but every culture, every period has its own beliefs in a power or beings beyond Earth. It's part of our humanity, part of our fiber to make up stories about superhuman powers. The trick, I think, is to separate the liturgy from the profoundly good messages of most, if not all religion. Ben Franklin said the Ten Commandments are pretty good advice. Even more so are Jesus' admonitions to love your neighbor as yourself and the idea of Christian charity."*

*"Yeah, and turn the other cheek, I suppose."*

*"That," the lieutenant had said, "I'm not too sure about. In my case, it's more part of my nature than any manifestation of belief."*

Mote was beginning to enjoy the show. Even though he had been cast as the bad guy in the movie, it was still fun to witness the twist in the plot, kind of funny really. *So, this is a good part coming up. The innocent, respectable school teacher has been scared by the nasty construction worker and petty thief — he was no friend, lieutenant; he was a pigeon and the biggest mistake I ever made — you come second. This one's not going to hurt as much as that one.*

The judge could not contain himself; stopping the furious light drumming of his fingers and his note-taking in a delicate hand, "Why then testify against someone whom you see as dangerous?"

"I had to. Much as I tried I couldn't tell a lie in court. It's a simple matter of respecting the law."

Mote shifted forward to look closely at Will's face, but Perkins seemed to be paying no attention to Mote or perhaps was studiously avoiding his old shipmate's gaze.

*Good and bad. Good and bad, Mote thought. Good I scared him, but bad that he thought I'm a murderer. Jesus, I don't believe I'm mad because someone thinks I'm a tough guy – nah, not someone, just the lieutenant. I thought he knew me better than that. Maybe he wasn't so scared after all. Here comes the truth. Yup, and that's what I should have known, that he couldn't lie in court.*

After determining that neither lawyer had any more questions, the judge announced that the charges against Mote of armed robbery would stand and the trial would be set for three weeks hence. "Take the accused into custody. Bail is set at 500 thousand dollars. Court adjourned."

Mote stood slowly and offered his hands to the cuffs. He looked for Perkins but he was already staring at him from about twenty feet away. Mote jerked his head to the side to indicate that Will should come to him. Perkins threw back his shoulders and with an obvious effort walked over to Mote.

"Coupla things, lieutenant, I had nothin' to do with the gunner's death. It was that ignorant deck ape." Mote smiled. "You were better than yourself today. I was happy to watch. No hard feelings, huh?"

"Hard feelings, no. Guilt, I suppose. Will you be all right?"

"Me? Hell, yeah. I live pretty well in prison. Remember that the cat lands on his feet, and I got at least five lives left. I underestimated you, Will. I'm kinda happy that my plans for you didn't work."

Will smiled back at this red-faced man with the twinkling grin, "I'm glad myself, Tim."

"Goodbye. You won't be hearing from me. You're no use to me."

"Goodbye." He gave Mote a sloppy salute, but the younger man stood at attention unable to salute with cuffs on. He watched Mote start to joke with the policeman and saw the policeman smile. He wished that he had more to say and he was unafraid.

## CHAPTER 27

# IT'S NEVER TOO LATE

Park station in Boston looks more like the gate cottage to an estate that it does a Metro stop, but on this day when Will emerged there was a low, murky cloud and the usual beauty of the garden was obscured by a grey light and light mist. He was drifting, but this time no tide was going to carry him into the Navy or into a change of careers or into marriage, but he was completely at sea. He was going to have to act and that was not his nature, much less his style.

Once again he wondered why such a talented and beautiful woman as Beth had married him, even though long ago he had come to understand. They seldom talked around their early dates and slide into marriage, and he had never asked her directly what she could possibly see in him, but he knew. He was safe. Even though she was very pretty as a college student, the reel running in the back of her mind told her she was plain, skinny, stooped, and undesirable. Academically, she was powerful and able to subsume any personal doubts beneath an air of cold intellect. Will was nice and smart and possibly more insecure than she so they grew comfortable with one another. Sex was comfortable and warmly delightful, not the thrashing event shown in the movies, and they could lead their lives with someone to talk to and be insecure around without any worries of barbs to their soft cores. No, Will knew they were a good match. After they had tried to have children and Beth's painful medical treatment, they had easily settled into their childless routines. But Mote shook all the routines and Will was both afraid and tingling with life as he walked toward Back Bay and their apartment.

The thing was, however, how to tell Beth. The last time they had talked seriously about children was fifteen years before when he had asked her, "Will you be very disappointed if we don't have children?"

"After all this," she had said, "the thought of just the two of us seems like a relief."

"I understand. We have a good life." Like most of their really important conversations, the words were few, but came after much thought. Now he was wondering, as he headed straight for the Fens to give himself more time to think, if he had been fair to himself with his laconic, conciliatory stance. Was he really happy with the thought of not having children even then? Or, had the difficulties just drifted them to an easy decision? Was there more that Beth had to say but had repressed beneath that professional exterior that only broke down when confronted with soppy movies or good ballet or a few glasses of wine? Will knew that if he continued to walk and think, he would arrive at his starting point. His mind felt like the mist and grey of the day. Time not to ask questions that could have, perhaps even should have, come up fifteen years before, but to actually confront and answer. The answer to what he was going to testify about Mote was surprisingly easy, but not so this question. Did he really want children above all else? Was he happy teaching? Was there anything missing in his relationship with Beth? No, was the answer to the last, but there was something missing in their dialogue about how to live the rest of their lives. How could he even begin that conversation? He would have her read his essay that he'd read to his students; no, he would read it to her and try not to let his voice betray his fear that she would turn pro and cross examine him. He had made his way back to their home where he began to take a mental inventory in the kitchen to see if he needed to shop for anything in order to make dinner. No, he had some squid and he would make a simple meal that they both loved: fried calamari, caprese salad, and spaghetti aglio e olio. All accompanied with a Soave. It would transport them back to their days of early marriage, which is perhaps where they needed to be.

When Beth came home, the smell of the garlic and oil worked its magic and she left Jarndyce versus Jarndyce behind and changed into jeans and an orange, cashmere top. The evening had all the hallmarks of comfort and routine after a day of no progress in the class action suit, but then there were the candles on the table. He only put candles on the table for very special occasions, so she looked to see what he was wearing – no, just the usual conservative grey pants with a blue shirt and red tie. No clue there, but he was moving too fast, almost dancing, and gave her a kiss, almost passionate, almost disturbing. Where was her husband? She poured herself wine and sat down with the *New Yorker*, which she hardly read but at least she didn't stare at Will who was now practicing juggling with three oranges. No, he hadn't been drinking because his juggling was as good and pathetic as usual. He set the table with the plates already loaded, took her by the hand to their mahogany table with a view over the Charles (if you bent to the left and leaned forward), and offered parmesan and black pepper, both of which she accepted.

"Any hint of progress on the class action suit?"

"Not a sniff, nowhere closer to discovery and the state's defense lawyers are claiming they're too overworked to even answer an email. Your babies okay?" 'Babies' was their pet term for the whining AP students who thought their lives were too hard and too devoid of enough time for socializing.

"Actually, good. They are really starting to find their voices and Charlotte is alive with ideas and experimenting with her prose."

"Methinks the lady has a rival."

"Methinks the lady has forgotten that the gentleman has already dealt with one brilliant wallflower and doesn't have the energy for another."

"Ah, but the gentleman has therefore made a comparison and thought the thoughts of a young man."

"Gentlemen of a certain age can only pretend to think the thoughts of youth. You look lovely."

Beth was completely caught off guard and her mouth turned down, not up, and her mind went to legal analysis of this uncooperative and digressing witness.

"And," he continued, "that was a compliment worthy of more than the legal frown."

She did her best to smile and look pleased, but both of them knew something was coming and that he was directing a scene for which only he had the script. He cleared the table quickly, and they moved onto the love seat in the living room that looked out the window and not at a TV, and he poured more wine.

"Mind if I read you something?"

She knew the moment had come, but had the sense of new evidence coming when there wasn't time to prepare a proper response. Probably a poem he's read, or something from the *Globe* about the parlous times ahead for American education, or maybe an essay from Charlotte. She looked for a hint and saw now that Will's hands were shaking, holding his typed pages. His face was flat, his eyes bulging – the look of an innocent afraid of the court. What role was she playing? Jury? Judge? Defense counsel? Prime witness? Gallery?

"The assignment was to write about the most important thing in the world. I wrote this essay as a model for the students. What do you think?"

Relieved, she felt her comfortable role as editor snuggle over her, until he began to read with a frog in his throat and a volume that showed he was trying to divorce himself from his words enough to read without overwhelming emotion.

As he read she was first intent, then surprised, and finally, when he'd finished, transformed from lawyer to the insecure woman who dwelt inside. She hugged him but was speechless.

"So," he tumbled, "what do you think?"

*Think? Think? Where can this be driving,* she thought.

"Sorry, I'm talking about adoption. I work half time and become a house husband and you become the senior partner who takes lunch in parks with her baby . . . Does counsellor need a recess to prepare her argument?"

"Well, counsel has introduced evidence that we have not had sufficient opportunity to examine. Will his sweet, lovely honor allow a reconvening tomorrow evening over dinner at the Four Seasons?"

She had dropped her guard and had shown the girl only he knew. He stood smiling his best smile, "Granted."

The Four Seasons was not only one of Beth and Will's favorite restaurants because of its refined service and exquisite food, but also because, with luck, they could look at the Common and enjoy the contrast between the European ambience and waiters and the hurly burly across the street.

Will was thinking of this contrast and how, in some strange way, the struggle between their settled lives and his broodiness was analogous to their surroundings. Beth was waiting for him, wearing a designer dress with Prada bag and matching shoes. While the outfit was not out of place in a law office, it was also right for the Four Seasons. The secretaries in the office complimented her on her look while obviously fishing for an explanation of what had driven her from grey suits to gorgeous colors. Their scuttlebutt minds were working overtime.

Will, too, was unusually dressed in a Brooks Brothers blue striped suit, more appropriate perhaps for Beth's office than his classroom, but he had tempered the look with a tie decorated with a ladybug theme. They sat quietly, ordered champagne, and Beth began.

"Do you think you would have written an essay like that marvelous sample ten years ago or even a year ago?

"No," Will answered honestly, "the topic would probably not have occurred to me, and I would have struggled with the idea of what is most important in life aside from you."

"Well phrased. You've got the makings of a politician."

Will grinned, "But now I'm thinking the essay may be truthful and spring from something inside that I think I discovered or that raised its head because of all this stuff with Mote. Does that make sense?"

"Absolutely." Beth was swirling her champagne, making it bubble, and feeling as insubstantial inside as the drink's bubbles. "Will feelings change now that Mote has gone?"

He was prepared. "Of course, I've thought about that. I don't want to pop analyze myself, but I think that the feelings in that essay have always been there. Now that they are in the open, they may not be repressed again. But this is no logical argument. Everything we're dealing with is emotion."

Beth stopped playing with her glass. "Not my field of expertise. Emotions are something to play with in others."

"But not to show. That doesn't mean the emotions aren't there just because no one can see them. I think maybe I saw something creep up in you when I read my little essay."

"Maybe. Maybe what you saw though was fear – fear of change to our comfort – fear of having to face all those insecurities that never show in my working life – fear of having to respond to the man I love with my heart and soul with no recourse to text or intellect."

"Well, Beth, let me be blunt. I think we're old enough to have a child and that we would be wonderful parents and love every minute. We'd have to adopt, of course. That's where I am," but he hesitated, "I think. Where are you?"

"Nowhere. Everywhere. What's the next step toward adoption?"

"Sorry, I really haven't done my homework, but I'm guessing we're a little old for the fast track."

"Slow, expensive road is more likely. Let's look at possibilities and think about what life we want from here on and maybe then I'll know how this new language fits."

"New language?"

"Yeah, like 'Daddy' and, for Chrissakes, 'Mommy.'" Beth drank her champagne with a gulp and looked over at a grinning Will.

## CHAPTER 28

# STILL WATERS RUN DEEP

If ONE THINKS OF THE adults in one's life, there are two sets of people we remember – our parents and some teachers. The classroom is, most importantly, not just a place where good teachers follow good pedagogy, provision well, plan well, know good classroom management, keep up with research, adjust lessons according to the needs of the students, use both formative and summative evaluation, and grade papers to provide avenues for improvement and not just to assign a grade. No, most importantly, teachers become a part of their students' private worlds and make students better than themselves.

In spite of his old fashioned dress and Spartan classroom, Will was also one of the few teachers his age who saw that he needed to keep up with technology; very few teachers had their own Internet account and he checked his that Friday morning as he did every day. He scanned the messages and lighted on one with a military address from a 1st LT Jerry Bowyer. Bowyer – athletic black kid, good mind, but lazy. Still, he was capable of real insight and his current students could learn a lot about voice from him. He opened the mail, "Mr. Perkins. I hope you remember me. I was just rereading *A Tale of Two Cities* (or a 'Sale of Two Titties' you once let slip) and I'm loving it. I thought I'd better tell you and thank you for saving my life."

Perkins, naturally, choked up. Wait till he told Beth.

He was late to class and there was the hint of a moan as he walked, or rather pranced, into his AP Language class. "So, you were expecting a sub today and instead you got me." He saw Charlotte shake 'no' with her head. "Well, let's see, what lesson plans did the regular teacher leave me? Oh, here it is," pretending to scrabble madly on his desk for notes, "a writing assignment." More muted groans. "The seniors have gone off to learn about graduation, so that leaves the real students behind." A few smiles, anyway. "You juniors will be applying to college before much longer so you need to start thinking about essays for college. Not all colleges require an essay, but the best that all of you WILL apply to provide a range of topics. Some want to know of difficulties you've overcome, some want you to evaluate your educations, some have open-ended essays, and the Perkins school asks you to write about a time when you performed a good deed or made a difference in someone else's life. Talk among yourselves for a few minutes and try to think of how great you are. Some of you will struggle with this, some of you think you make a difference in everyone's life every day and some," glancing at two boys in the back of the room, "will need to see if they can listen to others. Chances are you've already told them how great you are." Full-blooded laughter.

In a few minutes, it was time to write, and he had answered the usual questions about whether or not they could use first person (good idea, since it's about you), whether the story had to be true (preferably, but how will your reader know), and how long it had to be (long enough to tell a tale well). All seemed to be going well, but then Clarence raised his hand, "Mr. Perkins, please don't think I'm being a smart ass again, but I'd like to hear what you'd write about."

Charlotte looked interested but was also a bit worried that Clarence was usurping her imagined place as her teacher's favorite.

"Now, Clarence, are you trying to distract us from the task at hand?"

Charlotte pursed her lips and Clarence colored. "Well, no sir, I like it when you talk about yourself." So did the rest of the class and not one of them had pen ready to write.

"Sometimes it's best to state your idea in a sentence or two and then fill in the details. No details, but here's my summary. Over twenty years ago, I saved a powerful warship from a mutiny that could possibly have resulted in the loss of millions of dollars of the best weapons and technology in the world of that time and several lives. For my actions, I was awarded the Navy Commendation Medal."

Clarence was truly stunned. There were no teachers in his games but there were lots of cool military officers. "Damn," he said, "talk about still waters running deep."

The class waited for Will to upbraid Clarence for his use of profanity. Instead, he harrumphed a snort, "This assignment is not about clichés. TURN TO, CONTINUE SHIP'S WORK."

## ABOUT THE AUTHOR

LES BRYAN WAS RAISED IN Western Colorado, the descendent of Colorado pioneers. After attending Columbia University in New York City and Durham University, England, he joined the U.S. Navy, serving on active duty for eight years and a further twenty years in the Naval Reserves before retiring with the rank of captain. After receiving a further degree from Colgate University, he taught high school English in central New York for two years before working for the Department of Defense Dependents Schools, first as a teacher and later as a principal. He retired in 2013 and lives in Derby, England, with his wife Sue. They have two children and four grandchildren.

Printed in the United States
By Bookmasters